MW00529578

lesser american boys
zach vandezande

mason jar press | baltimore md

Cover design and layout by Ian Anderson.

This book is set in FF Meta Serif.

Publishded by
Mason Jar Press
Baltimore, MD

Printed by Spencer Printing in Honesdale, PA.

Learn more about Mason Jar Press at masonjarpress.com.

Stories

3   The Artist Requires Your Dissent

11   Reveal

15   Accord

19   In Ocala

25   Dad

27   Spite House

33   Status Updates

47   Tucumcari

53   Lost or Found

71   The Long Game

75   Luck

79   Full Bloom

85   Making an Illegal U-Turn on 15th Near Union

87   Imperative

103   Critical Theory

105   The Tyranny of "Critical Theory"

109   Duck

115   Flood Myth

119   Yelp Review

121   City Council

125   A Necessary Fiction

129   Kinds of Rubble

133   Walden

149   Social Animals

151   Hypotheticals

For Travis Hubbs. I'll keep going for you, friend.

lesser american boys

The Artist Requires Your Dissent

I took the job at the museum because I liked the idea of being connected to something that mattered. I didn't much get modern art—I had no gut for it—but I liked to think that there was something worthwhile about dwelling in the things that didn't make any sense to you. Plus I needed money. The woman who would be my boss liked my honesty. She had a lopsided smile that held something like warmth: condescension.

I became the outcast quickly enough. I wasn't an art student in the city and didn't have an opinion on Dan Flavin beyond liking neon. I tried telling them that I wrote, but they didn't care. I was just a guard. To them, that was the sum total of my ambition, and they were right enough. I ate my lunch alone in a little courtyard most days, staring at a sculpture of cubes stacked on top of each other that were slightly uneven. I worked nights on the weekends, since I had no place in particular to be.

I happened to be there when my boss was on the phone with the performance artist. I heard her voice: tinny through the speaker. My boss was wearing a clingy blouse that showed her prominent, bird-like collarbone, and her skin flushed when the performance artist said yes to the exhibition. I'd known a girl whose skin did that after a shower, after a beer—the blood pressed up against her skin at the slightest thing. I liked my boss right then a great deal. She hung up the phone and gave me a high five. She was chummy with me and not the others. I think she felt them snapping at her heels.

What surprised me most about the performance artist was how normal she seemed. I expected someone severe and unsmiling, some-one more like the art majors I worked with. When she wasn't, I felt ashamed. I thought that if she was famous, and if I ever had the chance to describe her to someone, it would be stupid to say that I expected someone severe and unsmiling. Like they would think I was some tourist. But it's what I thought when I met her, when she shook my hand with a firm grip, when she referred to the staff as *y'all*, when she said, *I want to talk to each of y'all individually*.

I had lunch with her in the courtyard, unsure of what to expect but not really nervous. She said, *What do you think your role is in regard to the art?* And I said some stuff that I thought I meant. Then she said, *Do you think your job is in some ways antithetical to the relationship between an artist and her art, or a piece of art and its viewers? Don't you think that a person should be allowed to approach art without fear of mediation or authority?*

What I said next is what got her to work with me, I think. I said, "I think art probably requires some misbehavior. And since my job is about making sure people behave around the art, probably I shouldn't have a job. Probably I am redundant or pointless."

She said, *How well can you keep a straight face?*

I said I could hold it together. In response, she pulled out a flask. And then, right in the courtyard, we got rip-shit drunk together. She told me about some of the stuff she had done. I told her about a book I was maybe writing about two people who keep meeting over and over again. She laughed and said, *Well it's nice to meet you.* The flask was whiskey, and I went back to work blanketed in its warmth. I stood my post, and when I caught her watching me from the next room, I didn't even wink. She watched me like I was a show dog that whole afternoon. I stood there, dumbly drunk, and did my job.

The piece was called "The Artist Requires Your Dissent." It was a bench, very much like the ones arranged in the middle of some rooms for the patrons, except this one was up against the wall and boxed in by black tape. She sat on it all day, inviting people to sit with her, to have a drink from her flask. She complimented patrons, or hit on them, or asked them what they thought of the art. She was charming and easy to talk to. My job was to stand outside the box and enforce the rules of the museum. I was to be kind, but firm and authoritarian.

I would say, "Please, stay outside the taped area," and she would scowl at me and tell them to ignore me. Persistent people would be asked to move along. Anyone who actually sat down would be ejected from the museum. For two weeks, I was the embodiment of everything that she thought was wrong with treating art as sacred, valuable artifacts instead of an attack against authority. She would say this to patrons that stuck around long enough. She would say, *Look, you don't have to listen to this douchebag. To enjoy art is to misbehave. Art should not behave. Not once. Art that behaves is commerce.* I liked to think she was quoting me a little bit. I would say, "Sir, you're welcome to listen, but I'm going to need you to stay outside of the taped area."

By refusing to cede her point, I was validating it. In this way, we learned to play together, to love each other. I've never played tennis, but it was something like tennis. The game required cooperation as much as competition.

At the end of each day, she would give me a long, warm hug and tell me how great I did. At first, it was almost motherly, the way she was proud of me. My boss would hug me too, sometimes, because the piece was a big hit. She was a bad hugger, her discomfort came through, but she did it anyway, which was a thing I remembered about her long after I'd spent what I made in those few weeks, which was considerable, and moved on to a different job. But I'm getting ahead of myself.

We worked in two four-hour shifts every weekday and one on Saturday. I still worked the night shift on weekends as a favor to my boss, who couldn't find anyone to cover them. Since we had the same schedule, the performance artist and I sort of fell in together during our free time. The other employees seethed about this. I felt my stock slip further among them, even though and because I was doing just what they all got this job to do.

We ate our lunch in the courtyard together, mostly sandwiches and junk food from the bodega a couple blocks down. We sat next to each other on the bench, and she started leaning into me when I would say something she found funny. Her laugh was loud. So was her affection for me. She didn't give a damn who knew about it, which I liked. It was during one of these lunches that she hooked a finger through my uniform's shoulder loop and dragged me bodily to the warmth of her mouth. We kissed for a minute, then she gave my face a friendly slap and walked off.

I've always been the kind of person who knew when he was in trouble but wouldn't listen to himself say so. I liked the momentum of trouble too much. So it's not like I didn't see things for what they were. Still, I went with her to dinner, and then I followed her back to her hotel, where I put my mouth everywhere I felt like.

The truth of what was happening between us didn't show itself at first. For the next few days we worked our shifts as usual while the feeling inside me built, and then we would sneak off to a bathroom or back to her hotel, walking quickly, each of us trying to keep pace with the other without seeming to. What we talked about after was buoyant and simple and unserious. It was easy to believe in.

It was only when, during one of our shifts, she patted the bench when no one was around, and looked up to me, and said my name, that I saw how I was actually drowning, that I had been breathing water for some time without realizing. I said, "Ma'am, I'm going to have to ask you to respect the art." And she frowned. And I thought: performance artist. And I thought about trust, how it relates to truth.

I was going to say something like, "What do you want me to do here?" but someone was headed our way. We went on with the show. I did my job for the rest of that shift and thought about how maybe everything is a game, or nothing is, or it doesn't matter what is or isn't in the end. It was all just gorgeous performance. None of it was enough, and none of it meant anything. For the first time, I wished I had an art degree, or something, anything really, to anchor me to her in a way that I could point to. And I saw, then, that I believed in the authority that I represented, which made me all ashy-mouthed and queasy. I wanted to walk off, but I didn't, which I'm still trying to figure out. When the shift ended we each went to different places. I thought that was the end.

It was a Saturday night, the last Saturday of her show, and I was at work, hanging out at the front desk and flipping through my keys, when she knocked on the door. She was drunk already, and offered me some from her flask before falling into me and doing something that was somewhere between kissing and licking my neck. I told her to wait, to let me catch up, and drank hard.

She watched me, and I asked if something was wrong. She shook her head and said, *Just that I'm me.* I said, "Me too." I understood what she meant, and I didn't, too.

We walked through the darkened rooms of the museum together, passing the flask back and forth. She asked me what I thought of one of the pieces and I said that I didn't much think anything about it. She called me a liar and walked into the next room. And maybe I was a liar. I looked at it. It was an antique dresser that had been set into a block of concrete. On the front, the wood was flush with the concrete, which filled what would have been open spaces for drawers, and the concrete extended out beyond the edge of the dresser, an oppressively large rectangle in the middle of the room. It was too dark for the plaque, but I remembered that the dresser had been recovered from a flood somewhere. What was sad about it wasn't its history, though. It was just that the space had been filled, and it shouldn't have been. I hated the artist for doing that. I couldn't decide if it was too literal or dumb or if I was, but something about it hurt. I wanted to cry.

Touch it, she said. She was leaning into the room from the entryway, the same way she had done when she was seeing if I could keep a straight face two weeks before. The next day, she'd be flying to a new city. I shook my head no. *Why not? It's yours, too.* "I don't want it," I said. I didn't.

I heard her footsteps, and her fingers found mine. She started talking, first to me about the piece, but then not to me, and not about the piece, but to everything, about everything. Her words filled the room, and it was prayer, or something like it. At a certain point, I let go of her hand, and she kept on. It all meant something, and she meant something, and I didn't know what. With each breathy word I felt further away from her, more inside of myself, more aware of my heartbeat and the sound in my ears all the time, until finally I was alone. I reached out to the dresser and pressed my palm against the concrete. It was warm, it was like flesh. It had to be.

Reveal

We're all at Bess's house and it's done up in pink-and-blue-construction-paper question marks, with crepe streamers loping along the front wall and across the fireplace, and Mylar balloons crowding us into the living room, and beads on every neck, and party favors and little bags of Jordan almonds strewn all over. The mini quiches are delicious and perfectly done and carry an air of quiet desperation. It's a lot, and it's a lot like Bess, who in college used to let us know that her half-birthday was coming up and expected us to care and/ or celebrate with her, and now here she is going to be a mother of a human and we are here to find out what kind. Most of us find all of this obnoxious or even offensive, either for the overdone Pinteresty self-indulgence of a gender reveal party or because we know better than she does about gender and the patriarchy et al. And some of us just have personal beef with Bess, of course, Bess being the kind of person who wanders oblivious through the universe and manages to irritate just by being, generally, a happy person. Anyway. There's going to be cake.

Bess's husband is around, but he doesn't really rate. Just a tucked-in polo shirt out on the periphery. And look, it's true that we're all assholes here. It's the suburbs. You don't end up out here by being thoughtful and uncompromising in your beliefs. But: it's time to cut the cake, and Bess is holding this big cake knife while her cousin, Claire Ellen, takes pictures on her phone and then on Bess's phone and then with a fat heavy SLR camera and then an Instax. Bess leans over dramatically and slides the blade into the cake once, twice, and then places the knife underneath the slice she's made. More photos as she lifts the piece of cake away, first Bess smiling, then Bess confused, then Bess with tears in her eyes.

Later, while Bess tries to not publicly scream into a cell phone and we're all eating a pretty delicious but undyed cake, we get to feeling bad. The cake sticks to the roofs of our mouths. Bess can be awful, but all she wants is a life with discrete meaning, which isn't that awful when put that way.

Bess gets off the phone, looking pitiable. The right thing to do would be to console her, to say it doesn't matter, to say the party is grand, and what's coming will be grander. Let her steal a moment or two for herself and her baby from the growing dark. We don't do that, though. We either look at her or make a point of not looking at her. Feet shuffle. Each of us has something to do with their hands, a drink to sip, a hangnail to finally rip free. Someone tells a loud story about diets, how they're hard, how nobody ever gets enough grace.

And who are we? Just the background texture of a story she'll tell, and it'll be either funny or an outrage, or else it'll ruin that little nebulous life growing in her in one of thousands upon thousands of small ways, the story of the first time the baby disappoints. Which can't be stopped. It'd be Bess doing it or someone else. It'll start here or it'll start in a little while or it's already begun. Things go wrong, and there you are, and that's being a person.

Accord

Rick Perry is on an elevator in the Statehouse building in Austin and he has to fart but he is not alone and he knows it will be audible and wet-sounding and of course he is also, at the time, governor. This is about a week or so after I drowned to death over at the Barton Springs Pool. Maybe you saw it in the local paper, though it wasn't that big of a story. It went like this: Some college kids on mushrooms broke into the closed park at night to go for a swim. One of them isn't as strong of a swimmer as she thinks. Drowning in real life isn't nearly the production people think it is—in fact, it's almost the easiest thing a body can do. It was a mental cut-and-paste job for the guy typing it up for the city section. Hey, presto.

Rick Perry is thinking about whether or not he can get away with letting out a little controlled fart, and I am dead by drowning. He does not know the people in the elevator, but they all know him. It's the first day of a new Senate session. My boyfriend of a month is sitting on his couch and trying deliberately to feel a little worse than he actually does about my death and the fact that he intends to use it as mental/emotional leverage to drop out of school, probably for good. My twin sister is at work repeatedly writing and then deleting an email to the guy who delivers coffee and other refreshments to her company break room every week. They're dropping him as the supplier in favor of employees bringing in their own coffee, and she barely has the heart to tell him. My mother is smoking a cigarette in the backyard of my childhood home, looking back in through the kitchen window absently. I am sort of everywhere at once, although it has occurred to me that maybe that isn't true, that maybe I am still in that moment of slipping under the water and my subconscious brain is trying to save me from the knowledge that death is an endless nothing. I try not to dwell on it, but it's hard. I've found it helps to focus on some kind of banal and emotion-free detail going on in the world, like Rick Perry's tightly pursed anus, that physical discomfort deeply rooted in the having of a body. A thing I would not possibly feel good about imagining to distract myself from my own death and therefore mustn't've, it must be really happening out there in the world, it must be that I am connected to everyone in my death.

Rick Perry doesn't remember me—at least, I'm not in his thoughts in any real or conscious way—but I remember him. He was speaking at a fundraising event, and I was there for extra credit in my high school government class. Our teacher wanted us to go out and get invested in politics. Like a lot of Austin kids, I was already invested. I knew Rick Perry as a man who wanted to control my body, who thought his slick-shit paternal authority was all that was necessary or valid in governance. I listened to him talk. I got in line to shake his hand. And then, when my turn came, I looked up at him with what I thought were my best big baby deer eyes and spat in his face. I was composing the moment, trying to be memorable and evocative.

What I didn't—what I couldn't—expect was the look of hurt, the loss of composure. I thought about it a lot while I did my community service, and then for a little while after, and then I tried not to think about it anymore.

When I think of that moment now, though, mostly I'm sad about trying to be remembered. It was a thing I did a lot, when I was alive. I was obsessed with being memorable—like, I would act almost as though I were composing the present in order for it to be a beautiful past. My smile would be brilliant, but not warm. I would be there but also in the place beyond there. My boyfriend, the one on the couch, said to me right before I went swimming, "You look at the world as though it's already ended." We were sitting on the hill leading down to the Barton Springs Pool, and it had just started raining a little bit. It smelled of petrichor, which is the word for when it smells like it just started raining a little bit. I was in that moment of being high on mushrooms when you are feeling at once that you wish it would never end and are also terrified that it might not, and I knew that word right then, petrichor, though I knew also that I had never heard it before. I said, "Hasn't it?"

What Rick Perry doesn't realize as he tries with an increasing amount of concentration to make it through this elevator ride without letting rip is that though, yes, his life and this moment is about him, it is also about me, and about the other people on the elevator, and my sister, and my ex-boyfriend, and that his struggle to not fart on the elevator is a basic admission that he wants to understand and love the people around him, and that, though he would say if pressed that mostly that kind of thing is just not done in an elevator—meaning it is a breach of decorum, which is one of the things he holds most dear when it suits him—what he is asking for from the people around him by holding back is the kind of unrequited and universal love that he can only provide for himself.

What I did was I stood up and stripped off my clothes, conscious of what I must look like but not really self-conscious that none of my friends had seen me naked before that moment. I walked haltingly down the hill, avoiding roots and slick mud, and leapt in. The water was cool, not cold, and I stayed under. There was just enough light to see the rough surface pelted by rain. I thought to myself that I could go deeper, that I could get to another, burdenless place, and all I would have to do was exhale. So I did. It seemed at the time like the only thing in the world to do.

Rick Perry steps off of the elevator and into an empty hallway and finally lets himself release a long, plaintive fart. It's the best he's felt all day. He smiles a little at the stupidity of his life. For a brief second, he's nearly a contemplative man. He's nearly a person I could like.

I wish I hadn't spit in his face, is what I'm saying. I wish I'd had the power to show him something more. I wish I'd had the power to tell him that he is compassionate in small ways, that he wouldn't fart in an elevator, which is a place to start. That he's trapped inside of himself and so is everyone else, and that his being right is no more or less being right than anyone else's being right. That there's very little between me and him and everyone else except the meat and bone that contains us. Even if it isn't true. Even if what I'm seeing in him now is just me seeing it in myself as my lungs burn and my body screams out for oxygen and my brain flips that little switch, the one that's been there all along, the one that's marked "let her think she knows everything. Abolish the concept of time. This is the last, last moment. One last burst of purpose. Give it to her. Just give it to her. Make everything, finally, all right."

In Ocala

Hard things were happening all over the place that summer. You'll recall it was the year Miami went underwater for good, which sent the state of Florida into a kind of prolonged chaos. Someone opened up a scuba diving tour through downtown. The rich people lost a little and moved to inland condos while the poor people lost everything and moved to some other doomed coastal town—a slow race to rural Georgia. We were with them for a time, you and I, though we only owned up to our low socioeconomic status when it was convenient or guilt-deflecting. We'd grown up in two-story houses, gated communities, and we were welcome back there whenever. We both knew that, I expect.

There was that squat little house we stayed at with all the palmetto bugs outside of Ocala. We'd fuck whenever the AC broke, because you said at least we should earn our being too hot. You were a really good bartender then, not that you were proud of it, and combined with my job as a line cook we did okay. When I think about that house and that summer it's like a record's fuzzy hissing. We were hopeful, maybe, or at least we liked each other's company. Seems the same now. And, yeah, you were annoyed that I was content with what we had, that I wasn't angling for better pay or to own some stuff from Crate and Barrel, but it seemed more like petty head-butting than anything.

I wish there was more of a story to tell about that time, but it was just lost time, living, which isn't a story until you take out some of the stuff that happened and call what's left whole.

Okay, then, a story. The neighbor kid, Josué, was up a tree in our backyard when I went out there one afternoon. It was that sandhill pine, the one with the low branches. I think you were at work—one of those times when you covered the dinner shift for your boss at his other restaurant in Alachua. I remember when I first saw it on a highway sign I pronounced it like a person sneezing in the middle of a hallelujah, and you laughed your native Floridian laugh. Anyway, as I recall your boss was in a bind over a bartender that quit, so you agreed to go the fifty miles and work some shifts in exchange for gas money plus thirty bucks on top of wages earned. At least, that's how you told it to me. After all that happened, I could wonder if it was the truth, but mostly that seems unhealthy.

I was planning to drink High Life on the porch until you got off, but then I saw the kid. I didn't mind him being up there—the fence between our houses was a low hop, and his yard was bare except for a vegetable garden his abuela worked on, her hunched back was all I ever saw of her. *Let him climb a tree,* was my thinking, *he's ten.* I waved up at him and he waved back, shouting, "Hey, Mister Ben." Which wasn't my name. His English wasn't the best, and maybe he was simple, I don't know, but in any case I didn't have the heart to correct him. Plus, what did it matter?

Anyway, he was up the tree, straddling one of the arm-thick branches about twenty feet off the ground. It was a good tree, sturdy, so I knew he wouldn't fall out, and he didn't. I decided it was fine to drink my beer in front of him, so I cracked it open and set up in the lawn chair—that old rusted-out vinyl one with the adjustable leg and head rests—on the porch.

I was out there a fair amount of time, two or three beers' worth. I had got to thinking about some Wittgenstein I'd tried to read, about language being as complete now as it ever was. Like, he said language would be just as total if the only two words we had were *this* and *there*. It didn't make a hell of a lot of sense to me. Like, the system ain't closed, dude. Still, I was trying for self-improvement.

Then Josué was shouting, *Mister Ben, Mister Ben*, and to be honest I'd sort of drifted off, so he startled me. And I rolled out of the chair onto one knee and was up and walking over to him. He was pointing at something in the backyard that jammed up behind ours that I couldn't see—the back fence was a wooden privacy fence, whereas the ones between houses on this street were chain-link. I told him I was coming and then I was over there. I poked my head over the fence and still couldn't tell what he was shouting about, except the neighbor keeps bees and they seemed more riled up than usual about something from the way I could see some of them over the fence. You remember her probably. The Haitian lady, Saraphina, in her shower-curtain dresses, gave us the honey one time.

Josué said, "Mister Ben, what do they do?"

And I said I didn't know, because I couldn't tell, but they were definitely doing something. I hiked myself up onto the fence to see. The hive stood off toward the middle of her yard, a squat little box painted white. But the bees weren't over there. They were all gathered in the fence corner, thousands of them jammed together in a hot thrumming mass. Some fell away, and some would return, but mostly they were packed in as tightly as possible. From where I was the sound was like, well, it was like something you've not heard, anyway, and loud and sort of ugly.

I leaned forward to see better, and my weight on the fence riled the swarm some. It grew larger, a little dispersed. The bees looked like one clumped thing, like each one was a cell in a body, which probably is about right. Saraphina usually parked her car on the side of her house, and it wasn't there. I yelled up to Josué that he shouldn't be in the tree with them riled like this. He whined about it but started climbing down.

I hopped off the fence and met him at the tree. "This isn't safe," I told him.

"Nada mas es abejas," he said, looking up at me with spooky brown eyes. He was more curious than scared.

"Go home, Josué," I said, and he looked at me like I'd popped his balloon with a cigarette. Still, he ran off, and soon enough I was out there alone.

I took a few steps back and hopped the fence all at once, like I used to do in my hooligan days. In Saraphina's yard, the bees stuck to their corner, but a few of them were winging back and forth between the hive and the swarm. I wasn't afraid of bees—I'd been stung plenty growing up, enough that I didn't much care. I knocked on Saraphina's door in case someone was home to take care of things. No one came.

The hive was pretty much quiet. There were a couple bees floating in and out of it, but that was it.

I went back to the fence. The sound was hard in my ears. I got close enough that I could see the individual bees. I tried following one, but it got lost among the rest. There was heat coming off of them.

What I did next, I mean, I guess I couldn't help myself. I kicked the fence, below and to the left of where they were. The bees took off as one and I backed off. They didn't come to me though. They settled back into the corner.

I kicked again, and again. The bees took off and ranged a little farther. I jogged to the other side of the yard. The swarm crashed against the fence like a wave, hitting low and washing up over the wood before flying back away. This happened over and over again. Each time, a few hundred would stay behind against the fence. There was a rhythm to it, the bees crashing against the fence and leaving some of themselves. There was pattern, a reason. Then some of them started to drop. Still, they kept crashing. They were beating themselves to death against the fence.

I stood there and watched it all happen. It took an upsetting amount of time. The swarm shrank as more bodies piled up at the base of the fence. Sweat slicked the hair on my arms. It was July, and the bees kept killing themselves. The sound of them started dying out. Then there weren't enough of them to be heard at all from where I stood. And then there were no more.

I stood over the bodies and tried to decide if it was my fault. The world was changing. Bees played by their own rules. Still, I hated you a little for not being there, like you had something to do with it. I was bad at things on my own. A born fence-kicker. And I thought I would keep it to myself, what happened, how I felt about it. I didn't even tell Saraphina, though I should have, and I lied to Josué when he asked me if I saw them die. I hopped the fence and drank more beer and waited to not be alone, waited for you. I thought about it for weeks, thought about telling you, maybe. Then that faded, too, and that was it, at least as far as the story goes.

And then all the rest happened, that night you came home crying drunk because you couldn't bear to hold it in anymore, what was going on between you and your boss. I remember I felt relieved more than anything, like, I was glad it wasn't me messing everything up. I was going to say so, and I was going to tell you about how I'd maybe driven the bees to do what they did, but your eyes were always so beautiful, even when you cried—the way the green in them would show through—and you seemed so earnest and visible then that I just let you take all the blame that you wanted and walk back out the door to stay at your mom's. Sitting there alone I got too drunk, and I remember the thing that finally got me over to having a cry of my own was when I thought of all those little bodies by the fence. Which I guess is a pretty sad way to end things if you think about it: my mouth shut, my thoughts elsewhere, keeping a secret in reserve.

But now I'd like to tell you, at least about the bees, so you know the story. I'd like to say *this,* and I'd like to say *there,* and I'd like to set you free if I can. I'd like to give you something like forgiveness. Something whole.

Dad

The father sits down on the floor near the bed and says, *Now I am going to tell you a story.* But then: he doesn't tell a story. He sits there in the near dark looking lost and breathing with his ragged half-drunk filling up the room. The daughter waits, staring up at him, her father who does not tell stories. Who is not telling a story now.

The room is lit by the slant of light from the closet door. The father entered the room with some ill-formed goodnight notion. Perhaps he thought inertia would carry him through. Now he is here on the floor with his little girl turned toward him and she is the most gorgeous thing he can imagine. The brightest star, and no words for it. No way to push this feeling out of himself and into the world. His daughter looks at him, tentative and waiting, and nothing comes. The father wonders if a bird could grow so fat with seed that it could no longer fly. And what would happen to that bird? Something terrible, probably. Gutted by some cat. Washed down a storm drain and starved by its gluttony. Connected forever to some patch of earth. Something fathers can't bear. Something to be avoided.

Finally, the daughter speaks up, saying, *Once upon a time*. But she doesn't know what comes next either, being small, having never felt the burden of planning out logical sequence and consequence. Embarrassment settles in the room and weighs on both of them. The father rattles ice in his glass, the daughter flicks the corner of the blanket that she's wrapped into her little clenching fist. And maybe this is now the story: that for fathers and daughters it isn't often easy. That to say we never really see each other is untrue, only that when we do, something makes us look away. A good story is one that sometimes has a lesson in it. The two of them sit there and wait for this thing they've made to pass them by.

The father knows he should be better at father. The daughter will know this, too, but later. Later, when she is grown, when her own child sleeps in this bed, later after much strain and silence has happened between this first moment and the new one and the father comes in again—perhaps fatted on seed—glass held offhand and that same sour-breath-whiskey-clinking man still, rounder now, yes, and frailer now, and all those old man things that happen very slowly and then all at once. And there, beyond the conception of a little girl sitting up in bed in the slantlight from the closet, way out past what that light can reach, is a man named Gary who wonders where his brightest star went and who these people are in her place. And is that the story.

Spite House

The idea came to me from nowhere, as many of my ideas do. One morning it was just there in my head on the drive to work. It was one of those ideas that kept hanging out in the back of my mind, gnawing on my free moments like a puppy with a new toy. *You should build a house. You don't know how, but you should learn. It makes a man whole.*

I think my brain might've been Ernest Hemingway.

Anyway, it stuck around for weeks, and it seemed more and more like a thing I ought to do. I tried to talk to her about it, but in this story she was the sensible one. We liked to trade that job, as it so often felt like a job. When I said to her at breakfast that I was thinking of building a house, she looked around our kitchen, twisted her body over the chairback to look into the den. Then she shrugged. "Seems like we already have a house, babe."

Of all the endearments, *babe* was the worst out of her mouth. She employed it as punctuation for her sarcasm or scorn. Like, *are you literally a baby?* Like, *do you need Momma's milk?*

Still, the urge lingered. When the weather turned nice, the idea made more and more space for itself in my mind. *If you start now,* it said. *Or now. Even now.*

When I started, there was no keeping it a secret, so I didn't bother. I rented a trailer and a dumpster. I filled the trailer with wood and other supplies. I bought the tools I thought I would need on credit. She watched me drive up from her spot at the kitchen window with no expression on her face, as though she wasn't even there looking. Then she stepped out of the frame for a time.

I staked out the whole front yard and then dug it out to up against the property line on each side and the sidewalk out front. The hedge-row kept me from getting as close to the original house as I wanted, but after weighing my options, I thought better of tearing it out. She loved those hydrangeas. I tried to do it right, set out the little pink flags at the edges of the large square I'd made, so that if I ended up failing, at least she would see that I was serious. I didn't hit a gas main like I feared, but I did have to have the cable guy out after I severed the cord with a shovel. A freak accident. I thought I'd moved it aside.

He and I had a long talk about permits, which I knew about but hadn't bothered with yet. He was wearing a light blue polo shirt with the company logo on it. He looked official, with a razor-knicked face. He looked also like a tattler. So: I bothered with them, the permits, which took a while. In the meantime, I framed and poured the foundation. Through all of this, I didn't see her at the window, and I didn't see her leave the house. I had taken to sleeping outside, or in my truck. Neither of us went to work. We were both involved in our own project—I was busy building a house, she was busy being not a part of my building a house.

I had a bunch of new terminology. Joist. Rough-in. Rat sill. I liked their hardness, their use. I tried them out in my mouth as I hammered together the framing walls. I kept time with them. Mantra, I thought, wasn't a good enough word for it. There must be a better one, some- where. I read manuals I'd bought from the used bookstore, webpages on my phone, looking for what to do next. When each nail was flush against its board I felt a little closer to something. I guess I was.

I got up early every morning and started with the dawn. I tried starting earlier, but the neighbors said they would have the cops out. I was out there all day, working until the sun was deep in the sky. It was gorgeous to see after a day of building. It seemed to me a reminder that nothing you do is ever pointless. Here it was, this whole time in the suburbs, the kind of sunset promised.

"Promised by what?" she called from the window.

I hadn't heard her open it.

"You should come see," I said.

"I can see it."

I scowled at her. She scowled back. We both thought our dark and shitty thoughts. Then I picked up my hammer.

I didn't see her for most of the rest of the summer. I lost weight, and my skin hung off me in places like pizza dough. I became a deep reddish tan that I'd never been. I ate PowerBars and oranges, drank Gatorade. The idea for the oranges was from when I was a kid at soccer camp, how they kept you hydrated. Of course, I didn't know if that was true. But it seemed true, and that was good enough. I had other things to be worried about.

One day, when I was framing the second story, a guy pulled up in his truck. He was wearing a shirt that advertised a local dirtbag honky-tonk. Underneath the name of the place it said, *a great place for dancin' and glancin'*. The only reason I mention the shirt is that I thought she would've gotten a kick out of it.

He asked me how it was going in the cadence of a car salesman or door-to-door missionary. I knew he wanted something from me. I had three or four nails in my mouth, point first, so I just shrugged and turned back to my work.

"You hiring?" he asked.

I said no.

"It's a good job you're doing," he said.

I nodded.

"But why, I wonder."

I ignored him.

"Just seems a man doing something for no reason is really doing nothing."

I told him to get lost.

He stuck around for a while, sat in his truck bed and ate lunch. Later she poked her head out the window. "Did you see that guy's shirt?" she asked. We had a laugh about it. She shimmied her shoulders, stopped, gave me a sideways look. "You think like that? Or both at once? Dancin' and glancin', or dancin' then glancin'?"

"Seems safer to do one then the other." I started up my ladder.

"Right," she said. "Safety first." When I got up to the second story she was gone from the window again.

Once the skeleton of wood was done, I saw how my house was going to tower over our house. It would block the sun from the afternoon on into evening. But the workmanship was good, and the frame solid, so I kept on. The downstairs walls were up before the nights turned cold, before fall went fully ugly and orangey-red. The man came around a time or two, but I shooed him off. I did it all myself.

The house was all walled in before Thanksgiving, the doors hung. I opened my back door, which stood a few feet away from our front door, and knocked. She opened it, blank-faced and waiting, and

I invited her to come in and see. She came out and stopped at the threshold, poked her head in. I saw that her hydrangeas weren't doing that well. *What a shit metaphor,* I thought, and then looked back at the house I'd built. The woman I loved stood at the entrance, one bare foot with its toes curled up over the doorjamb. She stood there for a long time, so long that *stood there* became *stands there*, meaning enough time passed without either of us moving that we caught up to now, to the telling of the story, and I'm looking at the back of her, wondering what she thinks of what I've done. Her hydrangeas will die from lack of light. The joints in my hands and knees ache all the time. Even so, I like to think that not everything is ruined about the world. I like to think I still have time to build.

Status Updates

In the new town she couldn't be seen by anyone, and it was better. No one who lived a few blocks over was telling another no one who lived a few blocks over that they were worried about her. No one was speaking their worry to absolve themselves of action. She walked the streets at dusk, and other people walked the streets, mostly with their dogs, and everyone was going somewhere. No one paid her any mind. She remembered as a girl wishing she was a bird, and now, here, she thought she might be. She smiled down at the dogs as they passed.

The bruises faded. Part of her missed them, thought it unfair that they would leave her behind like this. She liked better the way her wrist bone poked out a bit too far, the way it kinked where it met the hand. A bee landed on a dandelion at a coffee shop in the new town, and it was too heavy, the bee, and the dandelion bent to the ground. That made sense to her.

She got her own dog and spoke intermediate French to it on the couch. The dog looked up without lifting its head. *Je t'aime. Un jour, je vais être un oiseau. Un rouge vif cardinal.* His tail thumped the floor. Sunlight slanted into the room. It wasn't healing, but it was something like it.

She fed the dog macaroni from her fork. Sometimes they would run together for hours and then fall asleep on the floor under a ceiling fan. He dug out her garden one afternoon and she scolded him, and when she felt her voice pitch higher, crueler—when she felt like she might do anything—she ran to the bathroom and shook. She would not be her husband's wife. She would be new in a new town. She would be a bird.

———

The electronic sign read DRIVE CAREFULLY HURRICANE SEASON IS HERE. He had the time to look at it. He was stuck in a blear of baking traffic. Ugly as the sign was—and it was ugly, a bright orange with lightbulb letters rigged on a trailer, that government construction aesthetic—it seemed to him emblematic of something good about society. Horns honked. The sign blinked its motherly worry. Balance was achieved.

Later, after hoisting his toddler son up onto the kitchen counter so the boy could stack and unstack the measuring cups, he would turn to his wife and try telling her about the sign. But there was nothing to say. She smiled, waited, asked. He shook his head, and she laughed at him. Some things are so worth loving that you don't dare admit to it. Some things are already in the process of getting away from you.

———

A banging on the back door jerked her awake. It was early, or late, or just the time of drunken asshole yelling, which came after the banging. *Let me in. Mark. Let me in.*

It was her apartment neighbor's door, but it still sounded like hers, it still sounded like the beginning of a murder. Her heart went. She thought of the pepper spray in her purse, thought where her purse was. Then she thought of the kitchen knife she'd jammed between her mattress and box spring. In daylight, when she saw its vacant place in the knife block, she felt silly. Once, a date she had cooked dinner for asked where the knife was, and she made up a lie about the blade snapping when it caught in the dishwasher to avoid the shame of telling him. But she lived alone, and the world's ugliness would make itself known, maybe, someday. Her mother, like all mothers who read bedtime stories to their children, had instilled this readiness in her from a young age.

The banging kept up. She became angry about it instead of afraid. Now she kneels on her bed and lifts a slat of the blinds to see if she can see him. She gets a little slantwise view, nothing clear, but there he is, a greasy-headed barfly wearing a beanie in the summertime. A fool, even. He is leaning against the door, braced by one arm and pounding with the other. *I hope the wolves are coming for you*, she thinks, *I hope they eat you at the door.*

———

The transition, of course, was hard and emotionally and socially complicated. She was forever singled out by hesitant pronouns. Her first time going into the women's restroom—that moment seemed to be a clearing away of everything that came before, even if that stuff came roaring back later, often and at cruel moments. She'd lost family and friends over this, and even the well-meaning support she received came with unkind questions and comparative looks that reminded her that *you're not a woman like I am.*

A year later, she was starting to sense that she'd never feel like herself. Though she was closer, and that was something. In the meantime, she'd dated a man who said he was queer and said he was attracted to her, but she slowly realized he wouldn't touch her while he was sober. She'd promised herself and others that she would never deny someone their own identity, and he made that promise hard to keep, so they had to break up.

Today is her birthday, and there's a card in the mail from her mother. It's not a jokey card, like she used to get—it's heavy card-stock with words in cursive on the front. The card begins *To my daughter,* and there are flowers and little curlicues of pink, and she doesn't know what this feeling is, this new thing welling up inside of her, except that last year there was no card, and this year there will be a card but no phone call, and that maybe if she can hold on, if she can just make it, she'll find a way home.

————

He got so drunk all the time, and then he got into heroin, and then he fell out the bottom and didn't wake up. Poof. Bad magic. Some people didn't know whether to be sad or relieved. Other people knew just which one to be.

————

She spent her money on tattoos and wore long sleeves at work. It wasn't against the rules to have tattoos, but she felt a little weird about it. She was a tutor in a special needs school. The autistic boy she worked with kept pushing up the sleeve of her cardigan. His name was Cody, and she used it a bunch of ways. Sometimes *Cody* meant *you can do anything.* Sometimes it meant *you can't have popcorn.* When he pushed up the sleeve, his name in her mouth meant *no, but I love you a little more.*

One day, Cody threw a tantrum. He rocked and moaned and forgot what words he knew. She thought she'd like to live in another country just then. Some place where she could be more herself, or at least help people in a different way. Cody stood up and ran to the corner, and she went with him. *This little boy*, she thought.

She touched his shoulder and took off her sweater. On one arm were birds, thorns, a bloom of zinnias. These were her first tattoos. On the other arm were the more recent, more expensive ones that were based on artworks that she particularly loved. Kahlo, Matisse, Klimt, and the newest, just above the elbow, what looked like an oddly sketched pair of sunglasses with a face on one side and four line-legs sticking from the other. Cody liked to draw horses, and here was one. She showed him, and he looked, but it didn't stop his tantrum. Things aren't that easy. He hyperventilated, he dug into his arms for something better. Something, just something, he didn't know.

———

Stand there, look hard, don't smile. That's how he took pictures. The world was looking for a place it could put the knife in and he'd be damned if it found one on him. His girl pulled her phone back to them to look at the photo she'd taken and frowned, hit him playfully in the gut. *Act like you love me, god.*

Three days ago, one of his friends from high school was found slumped in an alley, shot three times, no witnesses. Now he was at a bar at the college town. Sometimes he felt like a spectacle here, or like he was on display. Noticed and watched.

He knew his anger invited a kind of trouble, that it was partly a measure of the way he walked through the world, the way the world treated him back. But, man, well, fuck it. No changing who you are.

His girl looked up at him all pouty, and he smiled. Like for real. Like there was goodness all over, and it was worth the while to put it inside of yourself and let it leak all over everything. She reached up and tugged on his ear.

Let's take another one, she said. *Show me your teeth.*

———

At night he can't stop thinking of the boy he killed. The boy had fired on his squad from a second-story window, hitting one man in the shoulder. He couldn't remember who because it wasn't a bad wound. What he could remember was creeping around the side, clearing room to room, and then the struggle as the boy knocked his rifle away. The field knife sliding in between the ribs. How he had to hold the boy in a bear hug, pinning the arms while the boy kicked and tried to squirm across the floor toward his Kalash. How he thought the boy was a man, until he was on the ground, when suddenly he wasn't a man anymore.

He's been transferred to a recruiting assignment. His new job is to go into high schools and talk to young men about a need for discipline. In a few hours, he would get up, put on his dress uniform, and look for the best and brightest, knowing, as his CO had told him, that he would mostly be settling for the sob-storied and luckless. He didn't regret what he'd done, and he looked forward to the job he had now. He knew that everything made sense, that everything clicked right into its proper place, and that the only danger left for him would be found in questions.

———

When she'd lived in Argentina, football had been the family event. Her father, especially, cheered the television. She liked most the way he would stare at the screen, a stoic, before suddenly letting out a burst of joy that couldn't be helped before resetting his face and continuing to watch, both hands resting in his lap. As he got worse, he would cough sometimes after an outburst. Then he got worse still.

She doesn't dwell. She sits there with her boyfriend at the bar and clutches at his knee when the strikers move in. He checks his phone, puts an arm around her shoulder, smiles. He is a good man, at least. A good sport, with money, and he looks good in photographs and is very kind. The bar erupts in shouts as the US team puts a header in, and she throws up her arms and yells, "You fucking Americans!" with no hint of an accent. Her boyfriend looks up from his phone, surprised and embarrassed as people turn to look. She sinks into herself. It is late in the game, and there's not much chance for the story to change.

———

The whole city seemed suddenly to be dissolving. Many of his friends were getting new jobs in new places, or they were marrying, which seemed about the same. While he used to spend holidays and Thanksgivings with these people, seeing each other was its own special occasion now. And it's not like he didn't have his own thing going on—he could feel himself coming loose from his hometown, too.

Buildings were coming down all over. A run-down Chinese restaurant near his apartment was a welcome removal, though the roaches crossed the street and hung out in his bathroom for a time. But then the bookstore was empty, and then the place where it used to be was made blank by bulldozers. Then it was the carnicería he went to. He thought, *Well, where did they go?* The bricks, the pipes, the people that stood in those spaces, the spaces themselves. The more he thought about it the more it seemed like an event out of myth, or like something was sweeping through and taking with it some of his knowledge. Like maybe next would be language, memory, his own physical presence.

Now he has gotten involved in a protest about whether a chain sandwich place should be allowed to rent space on the historic downtown square. They make signs, they sit in on city council meetings. Mostly they're good people. His people, maybe, but he still couldn't shake his not belonging. When they make signs, he wants to make one that says *I am not a ghost*. It seems to him that's the only thing that should ever be on a protest sign.

People somewhere are dying. Later, he will die, too. He sometimes looks on it with a kind of somber fascination.

———

After the rape, after the shock, after the corner-curled fear, after the questioning from wide-faced men, after the nurse tried to be consoling but didn't know a fucking thing about it, after the prescriptions and the drugsleep, after the looks at work that they didn't think she saw, after the too-long visit from her mother, after her roommate found a new place because *I really can't handle who you're being,* after seeing him there across the street laughing with some rail-thin hoodied nobody, just laughing, as in his life went on and he got to keep breathing without feeling how each insuck of air was a reminder of a body and a body was a reminder of a vulnerability and a vulnerability was a reminder of the pain of knowing that you are at once both a thing that was cast out of a star at a holy and glorifying speed and also just a cunthole to tear at, after all that remained the first and most forceful symptom of her humiliation: silence.

———

He climbs, he hikes, he owns a canoe and the thing he uses to attach it to his Jeep, whatever that's called. He likes best the feeling of no-place, the hush that isn't a hush but a different category of sound. She is a lot like him, except with a dog in a bandana and a Subaru.

They get married in a little church in the wood. Her mother is an accomplished and beautiful weeper. The ring bearer thumps his tail and pants. Everyone is happy.

They get jobs, good ones. A year goes by in the city. Then two. One of them is always comfortable with their life, the other is not. It alternates. Sometimes blame is assigned. The dog gets older all the time.

One day, he wakes to her crying in front of a sliced banana. She was making crepes with Nutella, a favorite, and then she was crying, and she doesn't know why, except that she is herself, the only one she ever gets to be.

So: they go to brunch at the fanciest restaurant they know that serves brunch. She is a little red-eyed, but smiling. To hell with the banana. They can afford it, and they can afford champagne, and they can afford being a little bit drunk on a Sunday morning, because they don't go to church, because there's nothing better in life than this or something like it.

———

He was at his most inventive while driving, and his inventiveness took the form of ever more complicated swears at the people around him. Cock wattle. Glass bottle squatfuck. Shitty itty bitty fuckstick.

Mouth-breathing dogcunt queef eater. He was more concerned with sound than with meaning, with how the phrase came alive in his mouth and bounced off the dash. He was not unlike a poet in this way.

He was deskbound at work, surrounded on three sides by neck-high, fabric-covered partitions. They were gray. It was call center work. He wore a headset, read a script, the same one every call, really, talking his way down an *if x then y then z* formula with angry huffing voices who wanted their goddamn cable to work.

Was it disheartening? It was. Did it leave him with a lingering feeling that he had not panned out? It did. It wasn't all bad, but mostly it was sorta bad. He had some buddies but didn't date. He had a father somewhere in Cleveland. He had a Nissan that he owned outright.

Hog stuffed cunt. Jizz smile slit lickers. Fucking crotch desiccants. He screamed them loudly, angrily, then couldn't help but smile to himself at what he'd made and how it felt.

———

That morning, as she was pulling it from its silk bonnet, letting it poof out every which way, having all that hair seemed like too much trouble. In two weeks she would be an aunt. In five she would graduate college, an art historian, if that was a thing you could really be. She felt fairly often that her wheelspinning would never start to look like an adult life, though she knew probably that wasn't true. Her married friends, her already-graduated friends, her careerbound friends—they all got drunk on Fridays, same as her.

She loved her hair, loved the thick tight curls, loved even when a white girl wanted to touch it, though fuck the white girls, too. It didn't stop her feeling proud. She scrubbed her hands over it and pulled a chunk of it straight in front of the mirror. Behind her in the mirror, a cheapie Chinese zodiac hung on the wall in reverse. Her hair had gotten long in the Year of the Second Housecat, the Year of the Baker Boyfriend. The Year of Not Near Enough Money. Now it was this year, The Year of the Horse, technically, and it felt like it, too, galloping right on by.

Everybody feels that way, she thought. Because they did, and because it bothered her, how much she often felt like she was trapped in the typicalities of her generation. The scissors sat on the counter, the first housecat wandered in, and she said looking down at it, "A haircut is a desire for more, for change, it's the most sincere cliché." The cat meowed back up at her, and she took up the scissors. "I'm probably in a movie," she said. The cat meowed.

———

He needed a meeting, but there she was, front and center like always, and he knew how that would go after the most recent split-up. Because she'd be talking about him, who he was and how he had enabled her. As he walked down Weaver Street with his hands jammed hard in his coat pockets he thought briefly about how easy it would be to turn left up ahead and score. Just a little something.

He put a finger to his mouth, got a hangnail between his teeth, and ripped it hard, leaving behind vicious wet and red.

Growing up he'd thought addiction was a physical feeling. Sometimes it was. Mostly, though, it was thoughts. And the thing was that they felt just like any other thought. And the thing after that was which ones were true, which thoughts? It all seemed so arbitrary.

Like the difference between her *I can't do this anymore* and his *No, it's that you won't do this anymore*. Mostly they're the same.

He wiped the blood on his finger inside his coat pocket. He knew better than all that. He also knew all kinds of stuff. Knock twice. Tell them you're up. The next street was the one, and he had cash in hand from clearing those tree limbs the day before, and if the meetings were her domain, where she would feel whole and supported by standing in front of other addicts and taking a hatchet to their life together like that was where the real problem was instead of stuck right there in her half-wrecked guts—well, his guts were half-wrecked, too.

He sat the curb and thought it through. Can't. Won't. No difference, really, except one's real and one's not. One is him. One is not.

———

His hobbies were making art and sleeping with people he didn't have enough in common with. Not even in that order. Meanwhile he racked up friends at his job, which took him all over the country. He liked the people in other cities better, and he fell into the habit of keeping in touch with a person from each place he went. He always signed off his messages with each person in a new way: *may the whiskey taste pretty good where you are*; *think of me when you reach your T stop*; *find some goddamn sunshine, Fran!* When he pressed send he always felt so full, or close to something. He wanted to feel that way more often.

What else? He met a girl in town, and by the third date she'd staked a sleepover claim on his bed. He let her. He bought the toothbrush. It was a happy time. They got along like gangbusters. She actually said that. She said, *like gangbusters*.

And of course it's fine that he keeps up with his friends in other places, and it's fine even that he's slept with some of them, and it's fine that he mentions her in his messages, and it's fine that he has his own inner life or outer life or whatever this is that she's found while using his laptop that has all of his passwords saved on it. Everything's fine, she thinks, as she tries to back away from accidentally logging in to a part of him that isn't private, exactly, but not her own. But she can't. She reads them all, or most of them, and she sees how happy he is touching these other lives, and she wishes she could be one of them out there, just to see what he might come up with to say goodbye to her.

Tucumcari

We looked all over for the wind because we were children and we were in love with it. Sometimes it even loved us back. We could feel it when it blew on our faces under a tree with branches too high to climb. The branches waved down at us, letting us know what the wind loved better.

A short list of other things the wind might have loved better: birds, newspaper, drapes, a dead locust.

Still, we loved the wind. It told us about our bodies. No one else was doing that for us.

On days the wind didn't come, we chased after ways to find it, but all we found were the imposters of running fast, arm flapping, standing in front of the grocery store doors when they opened. They were all something else, they weren't what we were after. We hung our heads out of cars, dog-lolling our tongues. Nothing we tried was the same as when the wind came to us. Then one of us jumped from a great height and our parents forbid us from loving the wind. We wondered how it felt for her, if it was real, what she'd found by doing that. But we couldn't ask. Our parents were keeping us indoors. They clutched at us and gave us ice cream. This went on too long—hugs and hugs and bursting bellies, while they fearfully watched us watch the windows.

What else: We ran away. We went west because we took a vote. West beat east twelve to nine on having the better wind. Out there were these great open fields where we spread ourselves out. One of us would call when she felt the wind, and we would hurryhurry over there, or we would take our chances with staying still if we were feeling lucky. Fights broke out over which way was better. A boy got a black eye over it, someone twisted an ankle running. We don't remember who. We remember the wind pushing the hair into our eyes and noses to make us laugh and squeal.

Storm wind! When we could find it, it was the best. The lightning licked too close, though, and cut up the sky. Canyon wind was punch punch punch, valley wind was nicer. Other-side-of-the-mountain wind was something, but then you got used to it and had to find another mountain. So much walking for children. Some of us cried and went home. One girl disappeared in the night, leaving her little owl knapsack. She loved it as much as a person can love an object that doesn't move, that's visible. We think something awful must have happened.

We reminded ourselves over and over that we were orphans now, for good or for ill, for the want of wind. We pictured our mothers being happy for us and missing us like crazy. We were so far from our real mothers that they were less important than the ones in our minds, which could be a comfort under the stars where we slept. Once, the youngest of us was crying into his folded arms about it, and an older girl put her hand on his shoulder and said, *Factual ain't actual.* Meaning we could be anything. And so we were.

When we met other people they thought we were spooky, a dozen plus children with no adult in sight. They weren't used to it. *Why aren't you in a classroom? There should be an adult, a school bus, something.* They looked all over for something that would make us real. We asked if they knew where the wind was that day. If they felt it, if they felt where it was going.

The warm-faced government people came for us, but we were faster. We could scatter. We were uncatchable wind children. Except some of us were caught, obviously, and shipped home to ice cream and actual mothers and long division problems.

After that, we lost the wind for a time. None of us knew why, if it was dumb luck, or maybe a phenomenon of the changing world, or if the wind had only loved the ones of us who were now gone. Some of us just thought we wanted it too bad. Imagining that someone could be to blame was a kind of comfort we held like knives.

The air was still all over the place as we ranged further and further west. The East Voters grumbled, the West voters kept their eyes on the horizon and not on us so we wouldn't see that they were afraid. One of them took a fist-sized rock to the head and had to get stitches. No one knew where it came from; no one was willing to say.

The youngest of us climbed a hill, closed his eyes, and spread his arms wide for nothing. He refused to climb back down to us. We tugged his limbs, pled. He kept his eyes shut tight and stayed put. We could not fathom it, this giving up. In the end, we walked on without him, some of us looking back at him. A frail, meaningless totem.

A ragged nervousness kept us quiet as we walked into a town of old hotels and banged-up parking lots. The paint was peeling from everything. Loose asphalt crunched beneath us. Fast food trash was pushed up against a fence, though if it was the wind that did it and how long ago, we didn't know. Everywhere we looked, sad-faced windows stared out at us.

We found an old pay phone and crowded around it to make phone calls. We called pilots, meteorologists, psychics, and storm chasers. Some of them knew some things, but never enough. Where were the rustlings and the tornadoes? The breezes and the gusts and the whistlings and the buffeting and what blows? We wanted all of it. All. We banged the pay phone's aluminum wall with our fists like hearts in tantrum and demanded answers, offering ourselves as ransom for just something that made sense and was whole unto itself. We were growing up out there. We shouted it in threat. Didn't they know we were lost? Didn't they know this was all starting to feel a little meaningless?

That's when I lost heart, if I'm being honest, while the others dug through a half-rotted phone book looking for someone else to call. I felt myself again. I mean I put my hands to my face and felt what the wind felt. I could see why it might have loved me. I was warm from the sun, and grimy, and I was twelve years old out there at a pay phone in an abandoned motel parking lot in Tucumcari, New Mexico, and when we left, I stayed. I closed my eyes and spread my arms like the boy did, not for the wind to find me, but so I could feel the edges of myself. That's what he must have been doing. It felt like there weren't any, so I tried some more to feel for them, to be sure. I kept feeling for them.

And then I was nineteen in that parking lot.

And then I was twenty-seven in that parking lot.

And then thirty-two.

And I was there, placeless, and realizing I was only something when I was on a page inside of a sentence, which is a kind of prison, too, I'll admit. But look: a sentence has wind. It moves and is gone again, and it's wind, and so are you as you pass over this word and this one and this one. And that's something actual.

The others kept on, the others found what they wanted, or they didn't, in the tornado, which is where we were always headed. They were knocked together and scattered and finally got to be the leaves they thought were loved best, while I stayed behind. I try not to think about how it must have felt like a betrayal to some—what the wind did to them at the end—but I do. I try also not to think about how I should have been there, how if I'd been stronger it might've been enough to save them. But I'm still here in Tucumcari. In the word itself. As in what's to come, what we carry. That's me.

Lost or Found

My friend Greg got run over by a street sweeper. It was unexpected. I told my girlfriend, Sarah, that he died of natural causes, which was in some ways true. He got hit, and his body reacted to it naturally: it leaked, it splintered and broke open, it stopped doing all the normal Greg things.

I don't know why I didn't tell her all that. Maybe I was protecting him.

I hadn't seen him in six years, since I moved from the place I had off Montrose in Houston, where we were neighbors. Now I lived in Eugene, Oregon, and rarely thought of him. In this way his death was abstract. I felt better equipped to grieve him because of the distance—I wasn't struck with the usual thoughts of *What about me? Why would he leave me now?* I didn't have to think about how he would go on those runs because of anxiety. I didn't have to dwell on how good he felt in being able to quiet his brain and focus on breath, or step, before the big machine sucked him under its carriage and spat him out the back end. I didn't have to take death personally.

What I would have to do is call Janelle, though we hadn't spoken in all the time I'd been gone. Sarah understood, but she wasn't happy about it. Janelle and I had been engaged once, for about ten minutes, right towards the end of our relationship. We quickly thought better of it. Sarah seemed to think Janelle and I breaking up was much sadder than it had been, that Janelle was a bitch who broke my heart. I let her. What can I say? I like being the hero.

Sarah said, "Let someone else tell her."

And I said a bunch of things I'd rehearsed. About how Greg had been Janelle's and my friend together, and about how Greg would reckon with an awkward phone call for my sake, and how the least I could do for him was make sure his not being in the world anymore was known as widely as possible. Sarah gave me her *you're your own person* face and wandered from the conversation.

I was antsy. The ringing phone. My fingers drummed along to the rain plonking the gutter. I was probably calling as much because I wanted to hear her voice as to share the news. Sebastian was the one who answered. Janelle's son, who at three had been a goofy little bean of a kid who liked yanking on my beard so it hurt. A kid who was just as likely to tell you he loved you during a hug as he was to jab a finger deep into your ear until it bled. He'd be almost ten years old by now.

"Hey, Seabass, is your mom home?"

He put the phone down without saying a word. I heard him yelling for Janelle. I shouldn't have called him Seabass like that. I was probably some stranger to him by now.

After some rustling, Janelle picked up and said hello.

"Hey, it's Thomas."

Her voice lit fire. "Thomas! Never Tom! How are you?"

"I'm okay. Older, I think."

"Me, too. I think." When we had been seeing each other, we spent a lot of time on the phone instead of in person. Sebastian was why—his dad was unkind to them both and had left her clinging to her family of two. Everything else, me included, was outside of that. We would get closer to each other for a time, enough that I would start to really see us as a couple, then she would back off, and we'd go back to just the phone calls. We got good at being on the phone, better really than we were in person.

"Probably." I tapped my fingers on the underside of my kitchen table. "I'm calling because Greg died."

"Fuck a dead dog, are you kidding? Greg?" She was blunt still.

"Greg. Run over by a street sweeper."

"You're lying."

"Hand to God."

"That's like, a Looney Tunes death. That doesn't happen." There was a pause between us. "What?"

"I guess there's just no way to shrug audibly. He's gone. Funeral's Saturday."

"Well, this is terrible."

"I know it is."

"You're coming, right?"

"I wasn't planning on it."

"Will you? You can stay here. I have the spare room."

"I don't know." I looked toward the bedroom where Sarah was clipping her nails on the bed.

"Greg's mom loves you, Thomas. Not seeing you, she probably won't remember that. But seeing you might be a comfort."

"It's a long way."

"Your presence is a present."

"Still with the wordplay."

"Sometimes clever and correct line up just fine."

Down the hall, Sarah switched to her feet, resting one foot up on the knee, peering close at it before clicking down on a nail with the clippers. I felt in a whole mess of trouble.

"I'll call you when I find a flight," I said.

Houston is garbage in the spring. Most other times, too. I stood outside the terminal smoking, though I'd quit years ago. Whenever I travelled I found myself slipping right back into it. All the cars driving by were dusted yellow with pollen, the only evidence of trees that were otherwise not much of a presence in the city limits. The air was thick and still. Sweat sprang immediately to life on my arms, slicked everything I touched. After ten minutes of waiting, my hair was damp and I felt beads of moisture running down my back. I lit another cigarette.

Janelle ran on her own time. I'd forgotten this anxious feeling that came with her lateness. In my worse moments as a younger man I'd thought surely she was late or flaky on purpose, as a way of letting me know my place, or keeping distance. Like most young men, I'd been skilled at being an asshole. Like most young men, I'd assumed people knew what they were doing. These days I wasn't so sure.

She veered into the loading zone in front of me and leapt out of the car before I realized it was her. She was roughly as I remembered—her hair was a mess piled on her head, and she wore an old faded shirt and yoga pants. All energy all the time, a room filler. That's Janelle.

"Thomas Thomas Thomas," she yelled as she threw her arms around me. I felt jostled more than I felt like I was being hugged. Then she held me at arms' length. "Look at you. Where the fuck is your beard?"

"What do you mean?"

"What do *you* mean?"

"I've never had a beard, Janelle. You're thinking of someone else." Telling obvious lies was one of the things I did when we were together. Once, I insisted that she pronounced pecan wrong, though we were pronouncing it the same way. *Pe-khan,* she would say. *No, that's not quite right, it's pe-khan,* I said back. This went on long enough that I started to feel mean.

She socked me in the arm, then and now. "You piece of shit." Then she took a deep breath and looked me over more closely. "I like it. Adult Thomas worked out pretty okay."

"Well, adult Janelle seems to at least have good opinions."

We got in the car. My carry-on was a fold-up bag for my suit that I'd jammed some extra clothes and a toothbrush into. I kept it in my lap because she hadn't offered the trunk. When she got in and sat down she turned to me and said, "Say something nice about me."

"What?"

"You haven't said anything nice to me yet. You're ducking all around."

She was right. I wanted to squirm away from this. Sarah, who I really loved—like, it wasn't a love of convenience or comfort or fear of change—was clanging around in my head, and I felt guilty being here. Though what were we doing wrong even? We were sitting in a car together because our friend had died. Janelle looked expectantly at me, her broad smile like a weapon in that moment.

"You're still you," I said.

"I'll take it," she said, and though there was warmth in her voice, she looked a little hurt, either because I wasn't playing the game her way or because she didn't want to still be her.

The drive to her place was filled with her voice, bringing me up to speed on things and people that I either couldn't remember or never knew in the first place. I didn't do much besides stare out at the idiot traffic, fiddling with the zipper of my bag. The one person she brought up that I remembered was our old pot dealer, who had been a sweet girl who kept a taser in her purse. She was the manager of a natural grocery store now. I wanted to ask about Sebastian, but she didn't bring him up.

She drove as though where we were going kept occurring to her. Sudden lane changes, blinker flicking to life at the last possible moment. When we pulled into the driveway of her little house, she seemed as surprised as I was. It was a nice place in an old neighborhood, overhung with shade trees that you rarely saw in this part of Texas. The suburbs of Houston trended toward slash-and-burn development, so most people's trees were about as tall as the people. It was one of the reasons I'd left—Houston, for all its great art and truly phenomenal restaurants, was surrounded by a deliberate and hard-won placelessness. I'd eat all manner of shitty enchiladas, which Eugene had in spades, if it meant knowing exactly where I was.

"Here it is," she said, and led me inside. The kitchen was hung with old portraits she'd bought at flea markets and painted over with glaring makeup and bright colors. There were also sketches of her nude figure—for years she'd made a little money here and there sitting for figure drawing classes, and the students often made presents of their work. They seemed to be arranged chronologically, starting with ones I'd known from before—her pregnant, looking tired with her legs akimbo. Her with her knees drawn up and looking away, exposing the arch of her spine, which the artist had left behind in guide lines. Her leaning forward in a chair, elbows on her knees, posed for all the world like a basketball player riding the bench. Then there were newer ones. Her in a yoga pose, one leg bent in front of her, the other bent backward, pointed up and toward the back of her head, her small breasts pulled taut in the arching of her back. She used to cup them and complain about how something so small could be so saggy and ravaged by motherhood. I didn't know how to tell her she was dead wrong about a part of her own body, so I kept quiet.

She saw me looking them all over. "I should take these down," she said. "Sebastian's friends."

"What about them?"

"I don't know. They're starting to look at me differently."

I shrugged, though I knew exactly what she meant. When we'd been together I'd hated these portraits as much as I'd loved them.

She stood by the drawings and smiled. "But they're me, you know? He doesn't own me, not everything. And these being up here remind me, and they remind me of him, too."

I shrugged again. "Seems like you're wanting me to either judge you or agree with you, but I don't know anything about it."

She made a show of giving me a thumbs down with one hand and blowing into her other to make fart sounds. "You coward. Come on, let's get you settled before I have to pick Sebastian up from school."

———

Janelle decided we would go get Sebastian together and take him for a snack before dropping him off at his grandma's for the weekend. She made a point of asking me if that would be okay. I went along with it. What wouldn't be okay about it? When we pulled into the line of parents at the middle school, I saw him—bigger than the other kids, a little husky but not unhealthily so. He would probably grow out of it soon, but not before some merciless teasing. I felt for the kid.

Janelle honked and Sebastian looked up and squinted towards us. I got out of the car and moved to the back seat. Janelle laughed at me. "What are you doing?"

"Letting him sit up front."

"He's ten. Plus, he's pretty much over me, anyway."

Sebastian got in the car with a half-spoken, "Hey."

"Sebastian, do you remember Thomas? He's Mom's friend from when you were real little."

Sebastian looked back at me. "Nope."

"Don't be rude," Janelle said.

"I'm not. I just don't remember him."

There wasn't reason to feel hurt. He didn't owe me any remembering. It stung anyhow. I tried not to let it show.

"That's fine," I said. "You were barely even a person when I knew you. I mean, you couldn't even read, you were unemployed, you didn't even have a favorite band. Things weren't going so hot for you back then."

He stared at me like I was an idiot. Probably I was. I stuck out my hand, and he shook it meekly.

"Don't mind him," she said to Sebastian. "Sometimes he's a real asshole, but he means well." She smiled back at me.

We pulled out of line and back onto the street, to the consternation of the volunteer mom directing traffic. Janelle slipped into parent mode, asking questions, getting curt answers. I sat in the back and looked out the window, watched the suburbs roll by.

I paid for the frozen yogurt, though Janelle half-heartedly tried to stop me. We sat at a picnic table outside, which faced out onto a parking lot and then a busy road. The whipping sound of cars kept our conversation to a minimum.

Sometimes I felt this thing inside myself, a feeling like I needed to say something but didn't know exactly what. It was a relatively new thing, something that came on with age, like my thinning hair. It had to do with wanting to articulate the central unfairnesses of being alive. Like I had the right, or some expertise that other people didn't have. Just then I felt it stronger than I'd felt it in a long while, and of course there was nothing real to say to relieve that feeling, so I just said something about Greg.

"What?" Janelle asked over the traffic.

"He was a good dude."

"Who?"

"Greg." We were shouting over the sound of a semi truck gunning it.

"Oh. Yeah, he was." She smoothed Sebastian's hair.

Sebastian attacked his yogurt with his fist-held spoon. A car pulled up in front of us and the driver got out, yelling into his cell phone. He called the person on the other end a stupid cunt before he looked up and saw us there on the bench. He went red in the face and held up a hand in apology before turning away from us to seethe some more into his phone.

"I'm tired of here," Janelle said, suddenly looking her age. She put her hand on Sebastian's shoulder and said, "Come on, baby, you can finish in the car on the way to Grandma's." She stood and looked into my container, which was still half full. "You too, baby," she said, winking at me.

After we dropped Sebastian off with his grandmother, who gave me a perfunctory, dry hug after remembering who I was, Janelle and I went to a bar that Greg used to like. Inside, it was dark and cold, and the décor was particle-board hipster stuff. They'd changed it all around since I'd last been inside. There was a lone TV showing a David Lynch movie on mute, and two or three other afternoon drinkers.

When Janelle and I had been together, we'd been dangerous drunks, the kind of people who would get obliterated and then wake up late the next morning to discover we'd been fired, or we'd lost a friend, or or or. Her mother agreed to take Sebastian once a week, and that was our chance to ruin ourselves as quickly as we could, but we also would often get drunk at the house while Sebastian slept. I knew by doing it I was helping her be a lousy parent, but I did it anyway. I wanted to be on the inside of something—after a few drinks *she and I* became *us*, a loose, warm thing where I felt like I finally had her attention. Being in a bar with her again made me nervous.

She leaned up over the bar on tiptoes and hugged the bartender, a woman in her thirties wearing a Subhumans shirt that had been crisscrossed with scissor holes. The bartender poured a shot of Evan Williams and pulled a Lone Star tallboy from under the bar. Janelle looked at me and I asked for the same.

She held up her shot. "To Greg," she said, and we clinked our shot glasses together, then tapped them on the bar, then slammed them back. Janelle let out a long breath and popped the top off the Lone Star.

"'He was a good dude,'" she said. "The most eloquent thing I've ever heard said about him."

"Shut up."

"No, really! Tomorrow a bunch of people are going to try and use words to get at Greg, and that'll be dumb as hell. Like, 'he was a good dude,' end of funeral. That's enough for me."

My phone rang, and I answered. Janelle walked off to the bar to give me space.

"Hey," I said.

"Hey. You get in okay?" It was Sarah.

"Yeah."

"Oh, okay. What's up?"

"We're at a bar. One Greg liked."

"What time is it there?"

"Two hours ahead."

There was a delay, a crappy connection. Plus she took a moment to respond.

"It's pretty early."

"I know. It's just a drink. Don't worry." Janelle looked over at me and I nodded. She signaled the bartender. "Listen, I've got a shit connection. Can I call back later?"

"Okay. Be careful."

"I will."

"Love you."

Janelle walked up with a drink for each of us. "You too," I said, and hung up.

For a minute we sat in thick silence.

"You remember his dog?" I asked, though I immediately realized I didn't want to talk about it.

She grabbed me by the arm. "Oh my god, Beater. What a dumb fucking dog."

"He really was."

She drank half the beer at once. "He died last year. Choked on something in the yard."

"I know," I said. "Facebook."

"Right. Gross."

"What's gross?"

"Just, we can't catch up because you're already caught up."

I frowned. "That's not true. There's plenty I don't know."

I kept getting distracted by the TV. It was *Wild at Heart*. Laura Dern's blurry face. I didn't like that I was distracted so easily, but then I thought about how it would have been useful once, when human beings were always about to be eaten by a lion. I would've been a hero, seeing them sneaking up.

"I like to think," she said, snapping me back to her, "I like to think that it was just quick, and he was happy. He'd set a new personal best, or he was running to a band he liked, their new album—you know how when you first hear a new album and you know already how much it clicks with you—and he was so excited and free, and it was one of those exhilarated moments, so good that even if he knew it was his last he would've said, 'okay,' and smiled."

She fell silent then and looked at me real serious before smiling weakly. I opened my mouth to say something then closed it again. I missed my friend was all.

We had sex in her car, desperate, grabbing sex. After, she got off me like a wounded animal. I'm sure I looked to her like a dog that shit the hallway. There was mashed french fry pressed into my palm, and I picked it off and let it fall to the back seat floor.

"I'm sorry," we said, though we weren't.

"Okay," we said. We weren't.

That's how what was always going to happen happened.

My suit didn't fit me anymore. I hadn't worn it in two years, and I'd gained some weight. Not much, but enough. The belt cut into my gut, the jacket looked terrible buttoned.

When we got to the funeral home, I led Janelle around by the small of her back. She let me. We'd slept in her bed, crowded toward each other by a pile of laundry. I had a missed call, an unanswered text on my phone.

Everyone looked old. Greg's mother walked speechless around the room. She was a large woman. When she saw me she wrapped me up, this great solid moment that had a twin from when I was a freshman in college. Then the funeral had been her mother's, and, as then, her grief was infectious. Or else it was a mirror of my own, one that I was avoiding.

Greg wasn't there. I mean that both ways. There was only a lectern up at the front of the room, an empty space, a wreath. Everyone sat down. Janelle put her head on my shoulder. People got up one by one and stood at the lectern, and I didn't listen because Janelle had been right at the bar the day before. Words can be the dumbest shit sometimes. We walk around all day thinking they can do anything, when really, the fact that anyone ever connects with anyone through language is more than a miracle. At some point, I got up and went out front to smoke cigarettes until it was over. I tried to think of what story I would tell about him, but there were no stories. There was just him, knowing him. My phone buzzed once, then again.

The funeral home, like everything here, looked out on six lanes of traffic. I smoked another cigarette until red-eyed people started walking out. I felt, among them, like a bored interloper. That was probably as true as it wasn't.

Janelle walked out with the phone to her ear. She had been crying, of course. She talked to her mother, then Sebastian, looking over at me occasionally to smile, like I was part of the conversation. I gnawed my inner lip and tried not to get close enough to anyone else that they might talk to me.

The parking lot had started to clear by the time she was done. There was talk of a caravan over to Greg's mother's, where there would be food and booze, and the cars were lining up. No one really knew why, since we weren't headed to a cemetery and we mostly knew where the place was.

When we were leaving the parking lot, she turned left instead of right.

"Where are we going?"

"I just can't. I can't go be with grieving people right now. They want you to do it a certain way, and I don't feel like being that way. Is that okay?"

I reached over and squeezed her knee. "Yeah, that's okay."

We stopped at a gas station and bought a case of Lone Star, then went to a liquor store for some Jim Beam. She drove us to a park and we found a concrete picnic bench to drink at. The park was mostly a soccer field, which was pretty well cared for, and some shade trees with patchy grass underneath.

We drank like there was a goal, a point of obliteration we were trying to reach by a certain time. We set the bottle between us and took turns. We shared cigarettes, swatted at flies and mosquitoes. There was no talking to do. She went to her car and got a junky towel, spread it under a tree. No one was around. She was wearing a short dress that kept catching the breeze and flying up. A pattern of sweat on both our backs. When I tried to stop her, she said, "Can there just be nothing else for a minute? No words, no context, nothing that's not this? Just this right here."

She rolled on top of me. In two days I'd gone back to years' old habits. My phone buzzed against the picnic table. I'd have to make up a story, some lie to tell about failing technology, a misplaced charger, a brokedown battery. Something to keep *this* and *that* separate. I knew already that I would. I didn't like being this person, but I was.

After, I thought about the time we dogsat for Greg. It was right toward the end, before I moved, the last favor I ever did for him.

Janelle and I were in couple mode, on that end of the pendulum swing when I was welcome in her home and we did most everything together. Greg needed someone to watch Beater so he could run an ultra in Austin, and I said okay.

I brought the dog with me to her place, though really I didn't want to. He was a shitty dog, always in trouble for something. I brought him because I thought Seabass would like to see him. And he did. The kid got all wired up and wouldn't go to sleep. He chased Beater all over the house. Janelle started drinking, and I started drinking. Then, while I was fixing myself another drink, I felt something on my leg, a body moving rhythmically. I was drunk. I thought Beater was humping me. So, I kicked out, and Sebastian, who was grabbing at my pants to get my attention, cracked the back of his head against the kitchen tile. I turned to see too late, and he was bawling on the floor. He'd bitten down hard enough on his tongue that his teeth and lips were smeared with blood. Janelle came in and panicked, and I said I didn't know what happened, though I did. It was an accident, plain enough. But I was drunk and careless, and that part wasn't an accident. That part was just who I was.

I never ended up telling her what I'd done. It's not that I was trying to keep it a secret. In fact, I'd meant to tell her the next day. We were at lunch, sitting outside at a coffee shop. I'd been building up to it, but she beat me to the punch when she said she needed to tell me something. She said she was late, very late—like, this wasn't the monthly paranoia of two drunks who were careless.

I told her it would be okay. I told her that whatever happened it would be fine, and I was here. She looked away then.

"I have Sebastian already," she said, to me, to no one.

"That's okay," I said. "I'll pay for half, or for all of it, or whatever's fair." I was hurt though. I was getting to the age where I wanted something of my own, something tethering me to who I was. I grabbed her hand. "I love you. You fucking know I love you."

"You shouldn't pay. This is my fault."

"It's both of our fault."

She shook her head, pulled her hand away. I knew then what she was saying. We'd always agreed that we could both do what we wanted, as long as we were safe. That it wasn't a relationship that had to put boundaries around who we were, what we had between us. I'd agreed to all this while not really wanting to, because I knew it was mostly about her past, her child, the things about her she valued keeping her own. I'd assumed the agreement was there so she wouldn't feel like she owed me anything, that it was symbolic. This was her way of saying that maybe it wasn't just about that. And even though that wasn't a betrayal, it was.

She wouldn't look at me. I didn't know what to do. That's when I asked her to marry me. I meant it. At the time I meant it. And she agreed to it. And I believed her. And then that was the last time we spoke face to face for months. She didn't answer her phone for a while, and she sent only terse text messages, and I let her.

And now here we were. I looked at her under that tree. Tomorrow I was flying home. The past was becoming the past again. The clouds overhead were going pink. A leaf blower moaned in the distance. Unfairness was settling in. My own, mostly, but also the world's. We lose ourselves for a second—or no, we actually become who we are for a second—and we end up hurting the people around us. Because we never listen to each other and ourselves, we never really see. I thought that if people could just figure out a way to stop hurting each other—and there had to be a way, didn't there?—then, well. I looked at Janelle. I saw her. A woman on a towel, her head up against a tree, her eyes closed to the world. I saw her. Probably I saw her wrong, but I saw her.

"We could've had so much," I said.

"Who?" She said it like she might be falling asleep.

I didn't know. "Everyone."

The Long Game

This is the long game: you eat of the fruit, you generation, you multiply, you virus yourself upon the land, you reach a point of real breaking, you feel alive and you are wasteful and then it ends. But you leave things behind. Little things. A satellite. A pyramid crumbling in the desert. Parking lots. A bullet lodged in a tree. Bodies that fell like *this* or like *this* or like *this* or didn't fall at all because they laid down and waited.

And look: life, the concept, is sad all the way around. Life, the particular, is something else entirely, but yes, sad, still so very sad. Have you seen a beetle scrabbling among stalks of grass? Have you watched a fox jaw-throttle its one-too-many pup? Have you sat with an infant waiting for the doctor to set its broken leg, or seen someone put torch to widowed bride? Or even just forgotten to buy coffee, or eaten a taco north of, say, Oklahoma, or been happy at the changing leaves before they dropped, while someone somewhere had a light that guttered and spit and went out for lack of care? It's all so much.

Why start here, you might ask? Why think of it on this scale? Why not focus in on how one person finds another person and there's love and then wanting and then wanting and then having and then more wanting? I ask, too.

Let's try. One person finds another person. They are not planning for it, but there they are. It's late autumn. They work together. They sit in each other's eyeline. In this way they catch sight of each other. One goes like *this*. The other goes like *this*. This is from across the room, and it's enough. Invitation in the very air.

Or: they have classes together, know all the same people, and before long they're a huddle in the corner of every situation, leaned in close, leaned in like it would shut out every looming paper, every student loan, and the kiss is electric, though yes, a little toothy, but they have all this huddled up time to get it right.

Or it's this: at a bar. A friend of a friend and there they are, two people tilting heads to hear each other over the Skynyrd, and why did they come to a bar like this, and won't it be embarrassing if this is really love, and this is the story?

Maybe it's this: oh, who cares about beginnings?

Meet cute. Meanwhile so much happening elsewhere. Meanwhile bombs lobbed and garbage filling up land and a coyote run down on the highway out west of somewhere, a car unswerving, a car undoes a special thing. Everywhere undoing. It doesn't go away when people fall in love. Try not to remember.

I want to pretty it, but not too much. The two have their romance and the world has its own romance and the things that happened between them happened in a way that was both kind and unkind, much like the world. And maybe they weren't in love. Maybe they were lonely in a system that would rather they were something besides human. Maybe they were scared. Maybe that's enough. I

don't know. I'm just here at the end, a satellite, a golden record playing on a loop—a voice, some brain waves—out here, somewhere,
hoping to be heard.

Luck

Once I was on fire. It was an accident (I don't want you to get the wrong impression). This was on the Fourth of July. I was drunk and a little stoned and in a beach chair on Jenny's back lawn at her barbeque with my eyes closed, and I was imagining that I was on a beach watching over baby sea turtles, shooing away gulls and these mean crabs and anything else that looked threatening. No sea turtles would die on my watch. Maybe I was half asleep, I don't know.

What happened was: his dog was at the barbeque, somebody brought it along, a real muppet of a dog, with thick, wiry fur that pretty much always looked dirty, and she'd found this old half-rotten tennis ball, and she was going up to each person at the barbeque and seeing if they would throw it. The ball itself was pretty nasty and had been found God knows where. Jenny wasn't the dog having kind. There weren't many takers, and the ones that did take the dog up on her offer soon found that she was a particularly single-minded dog. She didn't want to be pet, or her belly rubbed, or to play fetch with a stick instead, or to sit—she wanted you to throw the goddamn ball, and then throw it again when she brought it back. She was just that kind of dog.

She tried a lot of people before she got to Joan. I like Joan, genuinely I do. She's got a friendly face and lousy posture, which is a combination I can trust. And it's not like it's her fault that she really loves dogs, but her roommate's allergic, and so she tries a little too hard to get dog owners to notice that she really loves dogs so that they will remember her when they have to go out of town suddenly to attend a grandparent's funeral and she will get a chance to feed Banjo or Waffles or whatever this particular dog's name was. I don't blame her one bit for it. A freak occurrence. Couldn't be helped.

What happened was the ball was a little slimy and all from dog spit, so when Joan reared back to throw it, showing as much enthusiasm as the dog, it slipped loose, took an errant bounce off the base of a shade tree, and rolled to a stop underneath the still-live barbeque pit. It was one of those cheapie circular grills on three legs that Jenny set up for the veggie burgers.

You can guess how it went from here, I imagine. The dog careened into the grill, knocking it out from under itself, spilling live coals over the dog's back. Joan screamed. The dog's wiry hair caught fire, and she didn't even yelp, because she had the ball, and she was headed back toward Joan, whose scream sent her running away in a panic. All my drunk friends jumped and turned toward the sound. They all looked at Joan first. Me, I'd seen it all happen. I was watching the dog.

I don't know when precisely the dog knew what kind of trouble she was in—I still think about it, sometimes—but she kept running toward and then away from people, and the look in her eyes, and the flames rising off of her were too awful for mythologizing, and the smell, and the big bald cliché of a horror so inexplicably cruel.

No one knew what to do. Steven threw his drink. Mark ran away from the dog when it headed toward him. Joan kept screaming. I sat dumb in my chair wishing I were sober. Wishing there was something sensible to do when a dog is going to burn to death. But there isn't anything.

When the dog turned toward me, the wild flames rising off of her, it felt like I knew what would happen. She came close enough that I was able to reach out and hook a finger through her collar. Her momentum knocked my chair over, and even though my legs got all tangled up in it I was able to land sort of on top of her. I held her down as best I could while she squealed and bit at me. I knew I was being burned too, but mostly I held tight and tried to keep a clear head. I locked my arm around the dog's neck and squeezed as hard as I could. The dog stopped struggling, and I felt something give in her throat. Someone ran up with the hose.

Some people said I was a hero, but I don't know. I think they think I was just trying to hold her down or smother out the flames. I wasn't. It seems cruel and more than a little useless to try and correct them.

I ended up with some minor burns and a ruined shirt and some very awkward sex with Joan, which maybe isn't worth mentioning, but it's part of the story. The dog's owner, who I didn't personally know, slipped quietly out of all of our lives, probably as relieved and eager not to see us again as we were. Last I heard he'd taken a job out in Las Cruces.

Every year when the new grad students come to town, somebody sees fit to tell it again. It's always told a little wrong, just like every story. More often than not, the fresh-faced response is to turn to me and say that I was so lucky to not be hurt worse. I guess that's true: I was lucky. A thing I may as well believe.

Full Bloom

The first sign of trouble between us was the bombs. There was a homeless man on the news in one of those just-before-the-commercial segments where the tone is somewhere between puzzled and mocking. He said a shell had crashed into an abandoned factory without going off. She called me into the room to see because the man looked a little like an old college professor she'd had. The police officer they interviewed afterward said the bomb had been analyzed and that there was no danger. It was full of flowers. Probably an art project or a prank that had gone too far.

Then there were four bombs in a week that actually worked over different parts of town. There was the whistling sound, the crash, and then petals all over the place, raining down over a whole city block at a time. I was there for one of them, one of the first. I was in a coffee shop and saw these little white specks falling and getting kicked up by the breeze, like it was a ticker-tape parade. People on the street were taking videos and pictures. No one was hurt. No one was ever hurt. Still, we were afraid.

The mayor was on TV saying not to worry, but he looked a little worried. A spokesman from the city bomb squad was on TV saying there was no real danger outside of gravity, which struck me as a lot more thoughtful about the human condition than he meant it to be. A botanist was on TV saying this particular flower petal was an orchid thought to be extinct, this one a common peony, this one chrysanthemum, this one poppy, and this one silk, i.e. fake, i.e. none of his business. We watched them all, my girlfriend and I, the two of us on the couch eating spaghetti, while other people watched and ate spaghetti on their own couches, in their own homes. In this way we learned a lot without learning anything.

She took to going out with an umbrella all the time. "For luck," she said. She continued to say "for luck!" every time she took an umbrella for the rest of the time I knew her, which went on long after this thing with the bombs and all the remains of our relationship had blown over. It was a thing that I loved, even as I found it a little annoying.

The bombs kept falling through the summer and the people kept being on TV and we kept eating spaghetti without anyone coming forward to claim responsibility and without any kind of explanation. People had their theories. The president weighed in, even though it never spread beyond the streets of our little city. A guy I knew from down the block was on Fallon. There was a lot of nervous laughter.

Ultimately, she and I had to talk about what it meant. She said it must be a miracle, and I agreed, knowing that we probably had different definitions of the word. She said, "What's that old maxim? Show, don't tell? That's what a miracle is." We were talking about it in the kitchen while I cooked our dinner, which gave me an excuse to not respond. I didn't disagree, not exactly, but it seemed too pat and easy an explanation. I felt distant from her in that moment—saying so would have served to make the feeling true in a way I didn't want to deal with. I made as though I was concentrating on cutting onions. She leaned up against me at the stove and kissed my back, then ran her fingers over my shoulder and down my arm. I pressed against her with my own weight.

We weren't the only ones talking about it, of course. People on TV asked what it meant. Our neighbors asked what it meant when I bumped into them getting the mail. I overheard a group of college kids ask their bartender what it meant. My mom asked what it meant, her heart beating staticky and heavy into the phone. My dad yelled from the other room, *What did he say it meant?* Conversation got generally jammed up on this topic all over the place. More and more it felt like everyone was trying to suck the air out of something important. One night I said to her, "Explanation's a crackpot game," but I don't think she was listening. She seemed to not be listening a lot during this time. It bothered me, so I said, "Do you want to go looking for one?"

This was when the bombs were falling every day. It didn't surprise me in the least when her eyes lit up at my suggestion. There's something about the idea of a ground zero, about being there when it happens. Plus, she was jealous that I'd been there that one time. You could feel it in the margins of *how was your day* or *can you boil the noodles*. She never said so. She didn't need to. Some feelings, they don't have to be named to be known.

We weren't the only ones. Bomb chasers were all over the place, and they all had a system. You could see them in a coffee shop, or on the side of the road, carefully studying a map, a spreadsheet, the Chinese zodiac—whatever there was to guide a person, there a person was looking to it for guidance. The biggest problem was that there was no pattern aside from the fact that every blast site was within the city limits. So: we drove nights, from the time we got off work until she started nodding off against the passenger window. At times we were silent—I'm sure we seemed obsessed—but mostly we chatted and joked and ate spaghetti out of Tupperware.

As the weeks went on, our mood shifted. We became restless and sad and itchy. Picture Shackleton lost in the Antarctic. Picture a teenage kid realizing his dreams don't match his talent. Picture the two of us driving down the same goddamn streets, neither of us able to make a thing appear, me tapping away at the steering wheel, her hooking and unhooking the catch of her umbrella. I realized during those drives that there's little difference between the explorers, the seekers, and the lost. Going through it together was not exactly healthy for us. We got snippy more than once. I held it against her that we were out there, although of course it was my idea in the first place. She held it against me that we hadn't found anything. I held it against myself that she was holding something against me that I didn't have the power to change. In many ways, it's an old, typical story, which I also held against her.

When the citywide curfew came, it was a relief. We made a little show between the two of us of being outraged, then went back to sitting on our couch at night. That was pretty much the end of it. No more seeking. I knew it was a defeat, but I couldn't say how or what kind.

I'd like it to be that they never found him, that the concentrated effort between the local, state, and federal governments turned up nothing, and that the bombs full of flowers were allowed to remain a miracle, so that at least there would be that. But come on, you saw the news, you saw how often they repeated the video of dragging him down the court steps, turning him into just another guy with a lawyer doing his perp walk. So I have to tell you that they found him and that they explained it all and that in the end it was just a footnote, a Wikipedia page. To us, though, it was more than that, but—and I say this without any sense of bitterness or impotent rage but as plain fact—who gives a fuck what it was to us?

And that's one real sadness. The other one is this: She's in the middle of the street and she's wearing these green pants I never much liked and some thrift store t-shirt and she's holding her umbrella and of course the petals are falling around her and what are they but the confirmation that the whole human mystery will keep on no matter how much wading into it you do and of course the wind blows a little bit and a petal gets caught in the hair that the wind has pushed in front of her face and she smiles and in that smile is the same exact thing, the same meaning as the petals, and right then I would get the chance to realize that yes, all things are essentially worth doing, and one thing that matters is that she's not wearing a dress and the umbrella isn't lace and it isn't a moment so inauthentic that it basically becomes the new authentic, by which I mean that the moment I am describing is real enough to give me permission to not have to think about authenticity or truth or explanation or doubt or about my own perception as something that is both unreal and at the same time coloring my own reality, which of course means I am trapped in some heartbreaking keyless prison of myself, because the only thing that would be left to do when I see her there standing among the petals in the aftermath of what should have been a great explosive destruction is to stop and think, *Well what if I could have had it? The one moment. Okay? The moment, shown. A miracle.*

Making an Illegal U-Turn
on 15th Near Union

At a certain point you just have to go for it, and then you are hitting
the kid, and you want to say the sound is like a plonk, but it's not.
It's a sound outside of language, after all, and you feel that feeling
that you are part of the car, that the car is your body colliding with
the kid's body, and your own meaty body is just an organ in the
vehicle, your awareness of it proprioceptive—like a fender is your
limb and it is knocking the kid under and away. Not away enough.
The tire clumping over a leg at the kneecap. The soundlessness of
splintering bone. Think that a tire might be a cushion of air that
bears all the force, that you might be part of something misguided
but miraculous, before you hear the wail. Do not hear the wail. The
wail requires, and you do not have anything to give it. Ask yourself
what life meant until now and what it will mean after now. Wonder
at what point your belief in yourself as a person becomes insufficient,
and if this is that point. A bike will clatter under you, and here comes

the second rise and fall, the back tire adding injury to injury, here comes the onlook and the limblessness and the official response and then the shame-shouldered slump of the rest of your life. Here comes the new.

Imperative

It is night and the feeling is coming on again. You know the one. There are rules for dealing with this, a blunt methodology we have devised over time. Stay awake. Don't stop thinking. Don't let it wash over you the way it does. Find something to do.

———

The knight Wallace makes his way up the steps again. He holds a sword as long as his body. His face is hidden behind a faceguard. He is only steely determination. He is an abstraction of knighthood. It does not bother him. The staircase is massive, made of old, moss-mottled stone. At the top of the stairs he is flattened by the heavy warpick of a humanoid rhinoceros. A warpick is a weapon that has a hammer face on its end counterbalanced by a sharp pike, which is thematically appropriate for a rhinoceros. There is an internal consistency to this world. After a moment of blackness, Wallace appears at the bottom of the massive staircase. He makes his way back up the steps.

———

The feeling is creeping in again. Keep it in the peripheral. Don't sleep. Sleep is one place where it comes on. The feeling slides around the room, hiding in all the places it cannot be found. The feeling is clever that way. The feeling is a cockroach in a bathroom drain. A literal cockroach.

———

There is a certain austerity to phenomenology that we like. The world as navigated and articulated by blunt observation. Everything stripped of its meaning until a meaning is found. Phenomenology scrapes a brain clean. Plus we like the way the terminology rattles around in a sentence.

———

Wallace has a kind of resolve you admire. He knows he is alone in the world. The world was made lonely for him. In fact, the world exists in such a way that only what is visible is rendered. What the camera does not point at is not even there. It is a void, yet when Wallace runs toward it, he does not feel the vast terror that should accompany running full speed towards nonexistence. He sees only the instantiation of the real. There is no questioning of fate in Wallace. There is no asking if he has a will. There is only climbing the stairs, and what's after.

———

Sleep distracted if you have to. If you have to sleep, that is. Put on a show you've seen before. The one you like, the one that's a warm blanket. Or put on one you don't particularly like. It doesn't matter. Sleep drunk. Sleep with your laptop open. Read a website until sleep fights back. Put pillows around your body. Make a joke of it. Call it Fort Lonelyfort. Convince yourself you're not alone. Podcasts help. Music. Hours of pre-bed videogame playing. Put one unhealthy obsession in place of another.

———

The feeling is a lot of feelings, if you're being honest. Which we would rather you were not, so: do not be honest. Impose a kind of sterility of thought. Phenomenologize. Make an autoclave of your brain.

———

The cockroach hides in your sink, tucked in the overflow drain. Pokes its antennae out. It has all that it needs. There is moisture and scum. But still it wonders, if a cockroach could be said to wonder.

———

We strongly oppose attempts to sleep. If you sleep, you'll wake up, and the feeling will have you. It might be an hour. It might be five. It might be a gut-drop, body-jerk instant. Keep the feeling at bay however you can. Even as you know that not sleeping is a part of the feeling. Shh.

———

The feeling is the roach. The feeling is Wallace climbing his nonexistent stairs. The feeling is the worry that death invented time, that it wasn't the other way around. Death is impossible to phenomenologize. The inherent meaning of it cannot be found out, so any meaning in death is ascribed from outside the process of one's dying. And sleep is the cousin of death. We heard that once and knew it was true. So: don't sleep.

———

You cannot let the feeling find you. You cannot let the feeling up the steps. You cannot let the feeling gain any ground. Cannot.

———

The cockroach pokes its body out of its hidey hole. Darkness over everything—the toothbrush, the hand soap, the razor and the shaving cream. It climbs up and out, briefly on the lip of the counter, its legs splayed out on either side of it. Tests the open air.

———

The feeling is: you are maybe hurting in a way that requires professional help.

The feeling is: maybe you are not.

The feeling is: the only intelligent response to running full bore into the void of nonexistence is terror.

———

Here is what the knight Wallace is thinking: nothing! If only! Stoic is one way to describe him. Blank-faced under his visor. Or: no-faced. He puts his visor down and his face disappears. On the one hand, it's a matter of how a computer processor handles memory by not rendering what cannot be seen. On the other hand, it makes a certain kind of phenomenological sense.

———

The bowl of the sink is too slick. You have scrubbed it down recently. You scrub it down often, because the stuff that accumulates in the sink is the feeling. The cockroach slides down the porcelain and tries to clamber back up to its home. It is almost pathetic. Though you can't see it. If you saw it your breath would catch and you would back out of the room. It is the size of your thumb and scrambling nowhere. You are in the living room, living.

———

We know you named Wallace. Many times you are allowed to name characters in this way, to give them a sense of ownership or to invest them with personality. Do this whenever you can. We approve of your attempts to assign meaning where there is none. You chose, also, his armor, that visor, what kind of sword is best suited for the job. You send him up the steps and he is flattened again and again. The act itself is bulwark—a sacrifice against the coming on of the feeling.

———

You named him after another person, a person who you think sometimes felt like you feel now. You hope he did. A feeling shared is less intense. A friend you never met.

———

In the dark a cockroach is at home.

———

Do not give the feeling its name. Do not say it out loud. Do not admit a thing in the darkness where you sit alone. This is a hostage negotiation. There is a gun pointed at your heart. Or: the gun is inside your heart aiming out. We don't quite know where the gun is; but, the point is, there is a gun, and it's going to shoot something unless you cooperate.

———

The cockroach is nameless and you have no connection to it nor do you want one. But: it walks onto the porcelain of the sink, and it is too smooth to grip with the cilia on its feet, so it slips into the bowl, and its struggle in that moment can be said to exist in a way Wallace's does not. In a way that yours does not. It scrambles in panic and also in a sink. Its goal: get to the overflow drain at the top of the bowl. It knows of the danger it is in. Its goal: get home.

———

Elsewhere, other young men move their version of Wallace up the same stairs. They have different names, different armor. Some have axes or spears instead of swords. If it is a community, it is a messy or theoretical one. One built on difference and individual struggle instead of unity. They do not want to admit that their choices are meaningless. A weapon is a weapon is a weapon. Do not admit this either.

———

Watch Wallace as you are Wallace. An echo. A twinning of intent. A simplification. His failures are your failures. In this way, achieve a stillness of thought. Achieve something like peace. You are Wallace. Vice versa. Achieve seeing yourself as both, as a lenticular or a magic eye poster. Achieve not feeling the feeling.

———

The cockroach is also you. A metaphor of sorts. Though, again, actual.

———

Wallace moves up the stairs with grace. He dodges arrows that come toward him, uses a bow of his own to kill one of the archers. Three arrows. A health bar empties. The archer falls. Further up the steps he kills another with his sword after rolling under an arrow. Pretend you hear it whistle past. You are Wallace. Get to that empty place. Get smashed by the rhinoceros.

———

Log on to an internet forum to find the community. Talk about the rhinoceros. Say, "I keep getting my shit pushed in by that goddam rhinoceros." Get some tips, some sympathy, some knowing replies.

———

Do not say: all of this is inherently without value.

Do not say: I am afraid that I am utterly alone in all of this, and the mere acknowledgement of that fear makes it true. It is a meta-fear or a performative fear or the simulacrum of fear of a simulacrum and phenomenology is useless against it. It is knotty and empty and far worse than a rhinoceros on two legs with a hammer.

Do not talk about the feeling.

———

The roach fails to find purchase, unaware that the drain behind it leads to the same place, that it could retreat if it wanted, that it could move back into the shadows it knows without struggle. It runs a circle, a skittering mockery of draining water. It stops to suck some moisture. Its antennae twitch. Toothpaste, saliva.

———

Sit on your couch and pretend you do not exist. Put your phone on silent. We insist you eat cereal for dinner. We insist you keep people from seeing what a terrible fraud you are. We know things. We've seen that you are likable and kind for its reward. We've seen how brittle your humanism and empathy are. We've seen you cry at a funeral not for the deceased but for your own mortality. We've seen that every good thing about you is built out of something small and sharp and hurting inside of you. Obey our terms or else.

———

At the top of the steps, the rhino brings its warpick down hard, but Wallace rolls clear. Or: you roll clear. [You lock / He locks] on and [you move him / moves] to the right. The rhino circles too, jabs forward with the point of the warpick. Its armor is a beaten copper that's dulled and corroded in the fake sun, in the ages that it sat waiting before [you / Wallace] came to the stairway. [You move / Wallace moves] right, the rhino circles. Then it throws its crushing weight down on the hammer, missing. [You take your / Wallace takes his] chance. Two [taps / swings] of the [button / sword]. Blood mists the air. The rhino staggers back and raises its hammer again. [You deny that you are separate from what is happening on screen / Wallace dodges]. In this way the thing is done.

———

Sit on your couch and focus on the kind of struggle you can handle. Fall into bed at the last possible moment. Make sleep immediate, necessary, and vital. Ignore; ignore!

———

With enough time invested, the mind can become anything. Close your eyes and see Wallace. Feel safe.

———

Sometimes the cockroach thinks everything is too much because anything is too much.

———

Wallace lives free from desire. What he has is directive. Up the stairs, Wallace. Fell the rhino. And so he does. The rhino slumps to its knees, crashes down. The hammer clatters a ways down the stairs. Something like sunlight on everything. The doorway beyond glimmers. The goal is far taller than Wallace. Wallace moves to it, a great wrought double door covered in runes. With a hand on each door, he pushes his way in. The gate gives way. Behind, immediately behind, stand two more of the armored rhinos, too close together to divide and conquer. They must be killed as one. His world, cruel though it may be, is iterative. Knowledge of the system is leverage. It pays off. How nice!

———

You could be comparative. You could press your loneliness on to the figure that you control on the screen. What Wallace fights is the feeling. Or. And. Hm.

———

But the cockroach! You will meet it soon. It is there scrambling. It has been there before, out of sight while you brushed your teeth, avoided yourself in the mirror.

———

Wallace is to die again and again, each death meaning such an infinitesimal amount as to actually mean nothing. It's death that denies death. To actually die, Wallace would need to stop. You would need to stop. The real death in this case is a giving in, going to bed, uncoupling yourself from him and returning to the biological real and not returning to his world. Sleep is the cousin. This same struggle is happening in so many other apartments, irrespective of your own struggle, which is to say that Wallace's death is in some ways not inevitable in the same way as your own death. Letting Wallace die, truly die, would have an intrinsic meaning, would be a giving up. What about you?

———

You have to pee. Or: you don't want to answer the question we've put to you, which is fine by us. Go and see the roach. Go and flip the light and jump back and feel foolish for jumping back but feel disgusted too and feel a kind of throat-clutched dread take hold of you as the roach scrambles and scrambles around the sink and open the cabinet with your foot while you watch and reach down for just a moment while keeping an eye.

———

Wallace stands at the bottom of the stairs not thinking thoughts.

———

Hit the roach with aerosol poison. Never give it a chance. Let its respiratory system catch fire. Let it writhe and twitch in something like agony. One dead roach won't save you. One dead roach is knowledge, surety. A harbinger of infestation. Or: a fluke. An outlier. A wanderer who took a wrong turn and ended up in your drain. But it's proof of something you cannot contain. You cannot stop the outside from coming in.

———

While you stand there watching the roach die, we must insist: don't give in to the temptation to make this about you. It's so gauche, which makes us have to point out that it's gauche, which is also, all told, fairly gauche. Change particulars, deny that you are Zach and this is you playing *Dark Souls* because of something so bottomless as your anxiety, that black hole that doesn't have any weight you could name. Change details. Avoid specificity. Make it a mask so that you don't have to wear it.

———

Here's how the roach will get its revenge: close your eyes and it's in bed with you. Close your eyes and it's behind them. Try and think of Wallace and it crawls across the screen. Look at you. Defeated.

———

Now the feeling has barbs and can crawl around. Everything is a cockroach to you. Wallace is a cockroach. The feeling is a cockroach. And you.

———

Other people have words for the feeling. The feeling slides easily away from these words. Keep it in the realm of the unspecified. Do not attempt to hold the ocean with a teaspoon. Language is too childish, or: you are too childish to use it to describe this thing in you. It's a paradox, a head spinner, and the feeling is both a kind of confusion/lostness and a fear of that very confusion/lostness. But we're not saying that. We're not saying that we're not saying that, but we're not saying that.

———

The roach runs the bowl.

———

Try and find a shape for your life in the performative act of moving Wallace up the stairs. Though it is shattered, a mosaic. Hundreds of treks up the stairs as one seamless trip. There used to be a wilderness in you that you have evened out chemically and behaviorally, like stitching those failed attempts to get Wallace up the steps into the one success.

———

But language does have the words is the point. You have put them in your mouth. Anxiety. Ennui. Anhedonia. Fear. Cockroach. Gregor Samsa. Wallace. And you.

———

The roach runs circles in the bowl as the poison does its work. Bear witness in disgust. Watch as it flips on its back and its legs flail. Wonder: do they flip over to ease some felt pain as they die? Is it a letting go? Or just dumb reflex, some textbook fact of biology as their legs curl into their bent sarcophogal form? Do not decide on an answer. Allow that you are disgusted because a cockroach's being alive is mechanical and base, a set of imperatives in response to impulse.

Critical Theory

We got two Sharpie markers and went into the bedroom. The first thing she did was write *boyfriend* on my forehead, then she frowned and licked her finger and smudged the word around with it. "A terrible, nothing word," she said, and I agreed while she rubbed her palm firmly on my forehead to erase it. It felt odd being aware of the way my skin pulled around my skull. She wrote another word but wouldn't tell me what it was.

From there you might call it madness, the way we wrote all over each other's bodies. We put things we believed and things we hoped to believe up and down our arms. The feet and the legs below the knee were for verbs that we found fitting. Nouns went above to the middle of the thigh. I wrote *love* in the crease behind her knee and she laughed and said I was cheating by not choosing a category. A few things were crossed out, either by the author or by the person playing the page or by committee. When we ran out of white space we discarded our clothes and kept on.

Our backs were full of promises. Our chests had space for inside jokes and favorite memories and crude drawings of dinosaurs. I wrote the word *mine* on the inside of her leg where it met the tender parts of her and she smiled. It's what she'd written on my forehead.

As we wrote, we shut out doubt, that nagging thing saying, *of course the words are a prison of our own choosing.* The thought that maybe there was no way to really understand disappeared, redacted by the thick, felt tip. The words themselves were proof and reproof. What mattered was not *what* we wrote but *that* we wrote. Bodies smeared thick with black unknowing, each word already there anyway, already pressed into flesh before we ever got this harebrained, drunk idea.

When we were covered over completely with the things we claimed to know about each other, we tossed the markers aside and made love, giving in to what was beneath and above the language, believing the words to be true—how could they be anything else but true—but believing more that the best of all things could be told without words.

The Tyranny of "Critical Theory"

We got along fine, she and I, if that's a thing to be proud of. I imagine it's not. We held on to it anyway, two children at the same pant leg of agreeable politics, agreeable taste in music, agreeable bodies. It seemed at once more than enough and far too little. So: an easy, honest love between two equals, a thing fallen into.

The problem is that everything's a kind of artifice if you've got the right attitude, and hey, I had the right attitude. I was a midnight ceiling starer, a sucker stuck inside myself, the type of person to whom everything is either biology or pheromones or a fear of death or the scrunched-up pain of human history compressed inside of a word or gesture or whatever it is.

It wasn't fair to her, thinking this way. I knew she was probably starving. I was starving for something of my own self. And one night while we sat on the couch and watched shows we'd seen before, I looked at her and was just full up on this sadness of *how did we get quite to here?* A thing fallen into.

I'm not trying to imply that it's a kind of trap, but hell, maybe I should buy you a beer for listening so close. Because, okay, if everything's artifice then it all has equal value and you get to pick and choose and that's something like nice, or empowering. But then, once you've chosen, once you've really invested in something, the belief comes, and belief for a person such as myself is a poison, given that it's the same as pouring water into a bowl and then calling the water the bowl. Water, it spills and it's still water. But a bowl breaks and it's garbage.

I got up my guts and told her about all this. Her eyes shone. The ceiling fan was off balance and grinding at the end of each revolution. She seemed to really understand, which is not to say for sure that she understood, which ambiguity is a whole other part of the trap, which the trap is of course all the better for the fact that you never know for sure if you're in it or not. We thought about what to do. It took most of three nights. Eventually it was her idea we went with.

Her solution was to stay in that space of *Not Knowing but Finding Out*. We vowed to forget it all, to let all the hardened, known things about ourselves go. She said that at first it would be play-acting, but eventually it would start to take hold. In truth, it worked for a while. We were philosopher thugs, slitting the throat of knowing with tarnished jackknives, which is to say that we were sometimes casually betraying and then forgiving in equal measure.

But both those feelings were part of the problem, too, so we let them go as best we could. We had to avoid the trap of settling on truth, which meant never saying what we liked, what we didn't, never seeing who the other was, razing any sense of context or stability. We became animals, goldfish wolves, doing what we could and then forgetting. We were blank bodies, incapable of being written on or over. It was beautiful. It was something like beautiful.

She was better at it than I was. Eventually, it got to where she wouldn't even use my name. She seemed to react to me with genuine surprise whenever we spent time together, like I was always new. In this way we both got a little better at being ourselves. Sometimes I felt almost free.

And I can see you're about to say that a thing like that cannot possibly hold, that knowing something is like gravity, inescapable. She would say that gravity is just a coin that keeps coming up heads, and that tails is still right there, ready to show itself. Me, I'm here talking to you about it.

Sometimes I like to think that if we'd been stronger people, we wouldn't have turned so mean, it wouldn't have ended in so much ugliness. The silences between us grew longer, the cruelties stuck around, we got a little too uncareful with each other. Maybe that's just the way things go when you try not to know someone. Anyway, it was a mess.

It's pretty easy to figure out why I couldn't do it. She's another story. Mostly, I think she didn't realize, like I did, what the real problem was: what our bodies are made of is language. Not blood and gristle: language. It's a scary thing to realize that the body can form a question without your permission and send it out and away from you and then it's there and then it's out of your hands, which of course are just more language ready to be released. No matter how well she was able to embrace not knowing, our romantic idea was a doomed enterprise. Aren't they all?

Her body asked in every long silence: what kind of man is this? The kind of man who would carve little chunks of himself and give them away right on down to the bone and still feel it was not enough? The kind whose heart wobbles as it spins? The kind who thinks running away from something and running toward something are basically the same thing? Are you the kind of man who is mean, irrepressibly mean? Do you yell? Do you bite with words or otherwise? Is your life such hungry business that you cannot, for one second, stop trying to consume me, trying to take me inside of yourself in a way that mirrors my own warm way of letting you in but is careless and cruel and obliterating instead of an act of forgiveness? Or worse: another dumb animal braying at the fence, a ruminant. Are you knowable, or not? Her eyes said: tell me. Her eyes said: but not yet.

Duck

Nobody ever saw us coming. Bardo would get the gun in their faces, and I was already behind the counter turning the key on the register. We didn't even put on masks or gloves. It was that kind of bad town. We'd get the money, and we was out of there before you could say boo.

Bardo didn't feel no way about it, so he said, but after the rush wore off, I always felt kind of sickly. I even felt that way before we got into the habit of getting a little aggressive with the attendant, before that time I went and proved myself with the knife. Early on I tried to tell Bardo about it and he got me in a headlock, socked me in the ear so it bled. *Money ain't nobody's, you twat fuck,* he said. After he calmed down he helped me up and explained how this life ain't got no real meaning to it, and that survival was its own righteous imperative. Bardo had had some college once. I guess I sorta believed him, if only because he seemed so sure. Maybe I just believed the money.

I had met Bardo the way most people do—he put his gun in my face. This was at the Kwik Trip on Grand. He was running by himself back then. When he told me to hand it over I told him there wasn't any money in the register, that the smart move would be to come back at ten when Donny was around because he was bad at dropping excess cash into the locked safe. So Donny got robbed instead, and the next day Bardo came around asking why I did that. I told him the truth: Donny was a fuckup who kept saying things about this girl I was seeing for a minute. Bardo laughed then, offered me a smoke. Bardo laughs like a dog barks. It's got a rhythm and a threat to it, even when he's happy. He asked me why I wasn't afraid of him, and I didn't have no answer I could think of. I just wasn't. I didn't like my life, having quit high school the semester before, having not much going on besides weekdays at the store, and maybe that's why Bardo didn't scare me. We struck up a kind of friendship right there, out back of the Kwik Trip he'd robbed the night before.

From that point on it was him and me for everything. It wasn't long until he'd talked me into going along with him on a smash and grab. "Talked into" might be too strong a term for it. I wanted to go. We sat there in the parking lot before and he said, *You sure?* And I was sure. We got in there, and it was easy. It was just momentum—you only had to do the first thing, and everything else came after like gravity. For me, that meant just taking a single step back behind the counter. When I did that, I saw what Bardo meant about most things being just a handshake agreement. It ain't allowed, but you can just walk back there like it's nothing, and then you aren't even a customer anymore. You're something else. Until the time it went wrong, it seemed like what we were doing might be magic, the bending of time and space around what we wanted, who we were.

The boy I knifed said my name. That's why I did it.

Bardo didn't have much need for family. I guess sorta I did, and aside from my moms, who worked doubles mostly and didn't have the energy to care beyond making me box macaroni some nights, there wasn't a whole lot of family to go around. So: Bardo. He liked having me around mostly, I think, because I listened to what he said. Bardo loved to pontificate on truth and all its bullshittedness. I didn't much care one way or another. I guess I'd never had to think it through. He'd say something like, *most of what you see is being actively constructed. It ain't there except we make it there. All this stuff is handshakes and fear,* and I'd nod along.

One time he leaned in real close—this was in a back booth of that bar on State—and he said to me, *If it weren't for the wolves, we wouldn't have no indoors. We wouldn't have no society at all.* When I asked him what he meant, he laughed and snapped his teeth at me and said, *Ain't no value in wolves no more.*

He got me a fake ID—a real slick one, it even had all the water-marks and everything—and got me high on the regular, and we'd steal things when we felt like and then roll from bar to bar staying high and half-loaded on someone else's dollar. Seemed like Bardo knew somebody everywhere we went, but not well enough that they might sit down at a table with him. We didn't have no direction, but we had energy. At a certain point every night I felt full up with fire. Like I was sledding down the biggest hill you ever saw.

The night it went bad it was the same way—momentum. Bardo had his gun out and the kid hadn't seen him yet. He was facing the cigarette rack, picking at a crusty stain on his shirt, when we came in, so when he looked up, he saw me coming up behind the counter. And he smiled a little nervous, and he said my name like he knew me from somewhere, and I kept walking, and I kept pulling the knife out, and I kept bringing it to bear in front of me, and I kept, and I kept, and I kept.

Bardo had this game while we were driving around getting high where he would say whatever he was looking at didn't really exist. Like, *that McDonald's don't exist. That stoplight don't exist. That cracked-out woman on that stoop don't exist.* For a minute each time he even started to seem right. I tried it once, thought *that knife don't exist,* but it was still there slick in my hand like always. Since that night, time got kind of funny on me on account of some stuff I took and then kept taking. That knife was the only solid thing all around us, maybe, but I knew right then that Bardo didn't have the power to make right from wrong, to make a thing not exist. Maybe I'm getting ahead of the story. Things is confused.

Where did that boy even know me from? I thought if I could just remember then I could undo what had happened.

Bardo had a girl down the way, out in trailer park land. One time, I had gone with him over there. He parked me on the porch with a six pack and cigarettes and a laced joint and went in while I waited. From the way they were wailing inside, it must have been a nice time. I didn't know if they thought I couldn't hear or just didn't care, but this duck came by. An actual duck. And I quacked at it, and it quacked back, and they got real quiet inside. I thought it would be nice, being a duck. I liked white bread just fine. You ever see that YouTube about the duck that robs the convenience store every day? It'd be just like that. Get a bag of chips in my beak and just go.

Bardo came outside in unbuttoned jeans, and we smoked the joint laced with whatever and it was like my head was whistling on through the grass. Meanwhile, there was the duck. I talked to it, told it we was going to trade places. I wanted that knife out of my hand. I wanted to not be thinking, *well which of you was more surprised when it happened?*

We arrived at me being Duck now, Bardo and me. He grabbed the top of my head like a basketball and shook me around a little, brotherly. Then we went with his girl to some bar, where I watched him mash a boy's nose until it was a bag of gravel. I was sitting in a booth with his girl across from me on her phone. She wasn't upset about what was happening, but she wasn't going to grace it with her notice either. I watched him, though. I paid my closest attention. He was so powerful, so empty of unfulfilled desire. I felt myself stirring down there, which I talked myself out of being ashamed about by remembering the laced whatever from earlier. Behind him, a large TV showed a basketball game, but it looked more like he was framed by these kaleidoscopic colors. The sound of his fist cut through all the yelling. It wasn't beautiful to see, but it was something. It was then that time collapsed into a single sorry point in front of me.

What happens is, I grab a boy by his neck and pull him close, and the knife goes in, and we are eye-to-eye under buzzing lights, and we're in fourth grade together, and we're just two school kids on a playground, and we're playing four square with it just about to rain, which would mean recess would be called early, and the boy is mad that I'm taking too long in my attempt to palm the ball one-handed before serving, him wanting the game to be decided, and he yells, and I tell him to hold his fucking horses, and he charges me, and there's that too-common feeling of my body hitting the hot asphalt, and my teeth clack together, and the fist comes down, wild and uneven, and some teacher separates the two of us, both of us asphalt-pocked and seething, and the two of us grow into who we will be, him being gone now, me being Duck now, and that's about all.

Flood Myth

When we lived underwater it was a little better.

The others in our village fled up the hill when the water got too deep, or else they floated off. She and I tied stones to our feet so we could stay. A few others said they would do the same but didn't when the time came. Fewer still actually did tie themselves down. They all either panicked and cut themselves loose or drowned.

The first trick of living in water is to not drown. A thing you have to learn in a hurry or not at all. We set the drowned loose, but they stayed with us for a time. When they didn't float we became confident that we wouldn't either, as our lungs, too, were filled with water.

Above us, the storm raged on, and we were fine, just the two of us. We hoped to not be touched again by air, by rain, by some new storm that was more able to sting.

Would you believe me if I said we were happy? Well, we were happy. We had our home. Though the wood warped and split. Though the crabs hid in our bed. Though we could not speak much—we were made, after all, to communicate in air—and when we did speak it was big, shouted syllables that scared the fish away and were not, in general, understood.

The second trick of living in water is not minding it. The difference between day and night became barely noticeable as the sound of the rain slowly faded out of our lives. Night was a slightly deeper blue, but it didn't seem like less light. Soon, we forgot to look for the difference, gave up on time altogether. And we gave up other things, too. First the things that were impossible. Breathing, of course, but also pancake breakfasts, the knowledge found in books, clapping with delight. Then went the things that were inconvenient or seemed pointless, like shaving or having opinions. Soon, bigger things began to slip away. Things about ourselves.

A third trick of living in water is one the water plays: You are no longer yourself. She is not she in water. He is not he. It allows for a kind of isolated everythingness to being alive. Eventually, you stop feeling the boundary between skin and the water surrounding it. The body becomes permeable.

The fourth trick of living in water is that a human being can be not much different from a jellyfish. We took to drifting when before we had been obsessed with keeping our feet on the ground. It felt like giving up on a long-held disease. Our limbs took up new purpose and form in locomotion, steering. We slept tangled in the fast-growing kelp that sprung from the earth, bumping into each other if the currents made us bump into each other. When we realized we had moved away from the village, that it was lost in the murk beyond where we could see, we did not make attempts to return.

It was a letting go, and like all lettings go, there was no clear line between the sadness and the relief. But we were happy. We made love in new ways. We learned to rise away from the floor of our new storm-built ocean so that we could not see it or the surface, and everything was the same nothing blue.

And we stayed here. And there was nothing else but her. And I saw then that, though I was right—she is not she in water—what that really means is that she is finally allowed to be more, to be most, to be all there is or ever was. I was, too.

The trick of living in water is you can only understand yourself in relation to another. It's the end of narrative, of explaining, of the expansion of knowledge, which of course is just a limiting of that which is not known, a closing off of possibility. Telling a story is not just an admission that you're dying. It's the act and the cause of dying.

I tried to tell her this. She smiled and shook her head, her hair following slowly, and pointed to what must have been the surface. I could see that it was a little lighter than it had been before. The rain had already stopped by now. The rain was always going to stop. The sun was always on the way.

Yelp Review

We have a great capacity to make things into metaphors. One would think that some words are fit to burst, but they aren't. They can always hold some more meaning. This is like that one magic trick where the blond and smiling man pours a whole pitcher of water into a rolled-up newspaper, which is, one knows, a simile—the use of *like* makes it comparative instead of actual. One might contend that metaphor is also not actual but to do so would upend metaphor. One might become convinced of the too-manyness of blond children, each of them potentially growing into a blond and smiling magician. One might look at them and say, *those animals are not animals*. The point: a coffee shop in town outgrows its old building and moves, becoming, in the process, a new coffee shop (water, newspaper). It serves beer now, for instance, and has a high-windowed light and many, many outlets. To miss the old coffee shop in the face of this would be obscene. The exposed brickwork is purposeful, rust-red and new. The customers multiply, and the languor of the old coffee shop vanishes. In spring, the wind will catch the door, working it open and closed, ever ajar, the only difference being one of degree, like the building has breath. Seeing this, one might wonder where all the water went. One might miss the old coffee shop despite obscenity, or one might miss oneself. One might become convinced of two kinds of people: similes and metaphors. If one doesn't know what that means they are a simile, and if one does they are like a metaphor.

City Council

The city council, in a fit of anxiety and democratic governance, decided to open up the old air raid siren for public use. The general feeling was that in an emergency, there would not be time for nuance, caution. What there would be time for was a stomach-plummeting wail. The council was made up mostly of people who still watched the local news.

We're a sleepy town. The siren had been silent, except for a test on the first Wednesday of every month, for nearly thirty years. Still, most of us applauded the initiative, particularly because it made us feel that the little guy mattered, that he could be trusted to protect the community. A button was put outside city hall under a plastic cover, along with a little placard that said, "In case of emergency."

For two weeks it was talked about in the little coffee shop on the town square, and that was that. Then, one night, around midnight, Mike Evans went out there and put thumb to button. Sharon had left him, which stung. When the cops took him away he blew a .14, so even though he was within his rights from a public nuisance stand-point, they still dinged him for drunk and disorderly.

It sort of took off after that, especially once it got out that the town ordinance was worded in a way that made sure any townsperson's judgment of what constituted an emergency would be deemed suffi-cient. Everyone feels moments when they've had enough, when their inner life is crashing down, or maybe they're just scared, or found an odd-shaped mole on their back. And the button was there for them.

For the first month, it was sporadic, but often enough that we all took notice. At the next monthly council meeting, attendance was well above average (26 people, up from the previous month's 4, one of which had been a non-voting toddler). People wanted to know what the button was for. Not in general—that was well understood. But in the moment, they felt they had the right to know. A revision was made to the ordinance: Anyone could press the button, but first they had to write their reason in the logbook, which an enterprising teenager—the same intern who posted the town's weekend arrest mugshots to the police department's Facebook page every Monday—took to live tweeting.

From there, it took off. The siren would go, and we would check our phones to see.

Sylvia, who leaned on the button for half an hour, wrote: *because of my father, who justified everything.*

Artyom, who always said in his thick accent to call him Art, wrote in Russian: *I am here and not here.* It didn't show up on most of our phones, which couldn't display Cyrillic. Terry, who fancied herself a poet, said that it was all the more beautiful, our not even being able to see. Before her own blare of the siren, she wrote: *I always shy away from the long shot I should most take.*

Sharon, Mike's Sharon, went up there herself one day, saying: *f*ck that c*cksucker Mike Evans.* She censored it herself.

When Greg Dobson passed on, we let the mourners have their turn, every day at sundown for a week. The silence would be pierced, the birds would be spooked, and we would look to the people who were still around. For most of us, it didn't mean much—it was like a flag at half-mast, just sort of there. But that doesn't mean it meant nothing.

Then Billy McElroy went up there to lean on the button because his favorite TV show had been cancelled. He was a sensitive kid, a loner, but some of us called him a little shit, thought this was going too far. Those of us who saw him though, through the window of the coffee shop or on our way to pay off parking tickets, those of us who maybe looked him in the eye a little bit while his thumb went white from the pushing, well, we knew some things. There's a pit at the middle of each of us was our thinking, and who wouldn't lament the loss of something that made you forget about it for a minute or two?

A funny thing about when Billy went up there: he didn't put his name, and they let him use it anyway. This was a new wrinkle, and it broke the floodgates all the way open. Not an hour went by during daylight without the lonesome and tremulous blaring. And the log-book filled up with things:

Hope takes admitting to what you don't have yet.

We should love each other more than we do.

For Laika, that poor cosmonaut dog who burned up on takeoff. (We suspected Art on this one, but it turned out to be a young boy doing a research paper on space for school.)

This feeling I have didn't need a reason, so neither do I.

We wanted to call some of it overblown. We even liked the pun of it. But whose heart deserves silence? What isn't an emergency, when you get right to it?

And can you believe that we felt better? Can you believe something was sated inside each of us when the calm would break open, when the wailing went? Can you believe the city council member who championed the idea ran for mayor and won? And that we're happier, and a better community? That we learned to love our town, and, by turn, each other, a little more?

It's okay if you don't. In fact it's fine. Put it in the logbook. Press the button. We'll listen for you.

A Necessary Fiction

For a while I broke into people's cars. I mean, it wasn't a thing that I thought about, seeing as it was a sort of getting-by strategy that I only used when I got real desperate. I would say to myself, "Well, the world bares its teeth," and then I'd be out there in the night in some parking lot busting out a window with a screwdriver. When I said that, I was probably talking about myself, but also the world. Like I'm biting back, biting first.

Look, there's a problem in how good some things feel as long as you never think about them. When it was just me and an object and a sharp crack. Or sometimes just lucking out in trying the door. As much as I liked smashing my way into a car, it was better when the door just opened. The clean sensible feeling of that click, like maybe something better was coming for me, or at least I was more blameless, because whose fault is an unlocked door? Not mine, you know? And then I could picture them, finding fault with themselves instead of getting harder against the world. Just regretful about the dumb thing they did, then going out to buy some new CDs.

And so, when I had to, I'd go poking around these small apartment complexes on the north side of town. A lot of those smaller places, the parking's in back, and it's not well lit, and if people in the apartments see you out there, they figure you're just a dumb neighbor that they haven't met. What usually happened was I would drive by the place once or twice, then I'd pace around my living room for a few nights until I was fit to burst, and then I was just out there, suddenly, screwdriver in hand, getting hold of what I thought I was owed.

I should say that I never made much money from doing this, and none of the pawn shops would even take whatever I had for them, as most of the people who own pawn shops are the type to get wise to someone in a hurry. I kept doing it anyhow. I guess I've got a wolf in me.

The last time, the place I picked had about eight covered spots behind the building, and the apartments all had a little fenced-in patio that kept them from looking out and seeing me. I find myself out there, and I see that this car, this mid-size sedan with one of those *Coexist* bumper stickers, well, it's unlocked, and the door opens with that nice firm click, which feels good, and I'm in there, and I'm looking around, seeing if maybe the stereo is worth prying out, which it isn't, so I take the change from the cup holder and get out again to check the back. This is when I look up and she's there.

She's there with keys in hand looking all personally hurt, and I'm like, *oh shit,* and so I say, "Oh shit," but for some reason I don't run, and I don't even really know why, and I'm thinking like, *hey, you should be running; hello legs, nobody wants to be arrested today,* and finally I'm like, "This your car?" And she's like, "..." and I'm like, "I guess I thought it was mine. I guess I'm confused."

Does she believe me? No, of course not, but also yes, a little, but also the inherent threat of me standing there and of men in general, but also ultimately "okay," which is what she says, and I wanted, like, something else to be happening, something good, like maybe we meet and I say something about her hair because it's rich and brown and looks like it might be its own, alive thing, and she forgets for a second about the threat of me and of men in general and takes the thing I said as the world noticing her for her goodness.

Or even: we are together and don't want to get out of bed and instead we talk about dreams we've had that night and in our child-hoods, and her foot is touching my foot in the middle of the bed and she is seven weeks pregnant and we are both a little bit terrified but the moment is too gentle and sun-strewn for either of us to confess the fear.

I admit I feel a little lousy that this is the life we get, the one where I've opened up her car like it was whatever and then said I thought it was mine, which now strikes me as my true and honest feeling about the matter, which I didn't realize until her standing there made me.

I mean, I don't like being a wolf, I guess. But there it is.

I'm there watching this girl with her throat-caught breath, standing in front of me, and then holding out her keys like a gift or a cross against a vampire; i.e., me; i.e., the sharpened tooth of society; and of course I move from her car over to where she's standing; of course I cross that space and reach out and take the keys; and of course that's all it takes for two people to no longer be people. To not ever connect. And I'm all, *Well, man, I guess you've come this far.* So I get her wallet, too. An antique ring. A cell phone. Her sense of place in the world.

But what if this could happen: What if I could just say I'm sorry in a way that communicates my own weakness instead of the weakness of the act of saying sorry. Like I'm sorry for being a robber, not I'm sorry for robbing you. I'm sorry for this hard place we're in, I'm sorry for the world, for living in it how I do. I'm sorry for bad neighborhoods. I'm sorry neither of us get to be human right now. That it's so hard to stay human all the time. To remember.

And then the awkward returning of keys, of wallet, of other things. And the running off.

And which did I do?

This is where I tell you that the first thing I said, you know, "For a while I broke into people's cars," which implies maybe that this was in the past, was a lie, which I'm guessing you maybe saw right through. I like to think that I can't help myself, but probably that's not really true, because this was tonight, this just happened, and in a way it's still happening, and now I don't know which thing it is that I did. I'm so full of things I can't seem to remember. I need to tell them all. And it's not like it doesn't matter to who, but maybe that's true, maybe it doesn't matter, except that they listen, but I'm starting to notice that you look a little like her, or: you are her. Like truly her, and I'm here deciding, and also back there deciding, and this is the story. I want to put myself aside—the fear in me, and the threat—I want to be done with it. I want you to not be looking at me like that, and I want to deserve you not looking at me like that. Mostly I just need to be telling, to have it told. And then maybe you can decide for me what I did.

Kinds of Rubble

Our childlessness sat between us like a rock for stoving heads in. It was the biggest one we'd seen. We were eating dinner and then there it was, white and glistening like all the others that had formed in our home. I knew if I picked it up that it would be cold and wet in my hand, like a hailstone, but that it wouldn't melt. It was the second week of this.

The first one I found was in the garage. I was sanding an old barstool that I intended to paint, and when I turned around it was there on the ground: that apartment I liked in Sacramento, the one that she thought was too large, too high-ceilinged. She wanted to feel cozy, which I understood. But now here was this thing on the garage floor, a small disappointment made manifest, corporeal. I picked it up and held it up to the light. It was opaque. I didn't feel any particular way about it. Just: there it was.

When she walked in to ask if I needed anything from the grocery store, I palmed it, casually slipped it into my pocket. I did not need anything from the grocery store. Maybe some craft beer if one struck her eye. I was thankful for her asking me. I was thankful for so many things.

Why put it in my pocket, though? Why hide it? I couldn't say.

There were others after that. Mostly small ones. The year she got me a bad birthday gift sat on the bedroom dresser. It wasn't that I didn't like the sweater. I just didn't wear sweaters ever, and the gift seemed like a subtle complaint more than anything. Her coming in late—two hours late—without a call first, when I'd cooked her a nice dinner. I found that one perched on the lip of the toilet. I turned on the ceiling fan, and a pebble-sized piece—the way she folds towels too haphazardly—struck the living room wall, plonking the plaster, leaving a mark. I hid them all in a Crown Royal bag, the same way I'd hidden my 5-ticket items from the Chuck E. Cheese as a child, and stuffed it in my toolbox. The bag didn't get wet, it didn't feel cold from the outside. The pieces only felt wet and cold against the skin. If you shook them around they sounded just like rocks or marbles.

And then, during dinner, that first big one showed up—our child-lessness. We looked at it and each other. She had some sauce dribbled on her chin. I'd made the meal. But who cared about any of that.

After a moment she stood and went into the bedroom. She came back out with a wooden box inlaid with dragonflies that she'd got in college on a trip to Asia. Inside were more of them, ones I didn't recognize. To me they just looked like ice, mica. I went to the garage and retrieved mine, spread them out in front of me.

"I don't know what those are," she said, pointing at mine. I said about the same.

She held up one that was about the size of her thumb. "This is all those shitty bands you listen to in the car."

I held up one of my own. "Fingernail clippings on the coffee table."

She held one up. "Also fingernail clippings, just on the bathroom floor."

I couldn't help smiling. "Mine's worse. And you've got pasta sauce on your chin."

"Well," she wiped her face. "This one's how nothing you own has a place to put it, how you just leave everything in piles. And this is that time at the zoo. This is when you didn't call the cable company for two months after I told you to, how it seems like you'd rather pay forty dollars a month indefinitely than make one tedious phone call."

I told her some more of mine. I thought it wasn't that bad. They were so small. They weren't millstones, and this wasn't what drowning looked like. It was almost nice.

"This one I don't want to talk about," she said, holding up one that seemed flecked with gray.

"Why not?"

"Because it's silly. It's stupid. And it's not even true."

"You can tell me anyway." I didn't know if that was how I really felt about it. Faith in yourself is important.

She hesitated, gave a small smile. "I was at your office, in the lobby. I was waiting on you to come down. And I heard someone talking about you, a woman. And it was like in that moment she knew you better than I did. Which isn't true, and isn't your fault, and is gross of me, and I know that already, so you don't have to get into it."

I'd never done anything to betray my wife, but that I knew exactly who she was talking about was probably betrayal enough. In response, I held up a piece of my own. "This is Troy. Just all of him, every little shitty thing about him. So we're both petty. It's even."

And it was. We counted up the pieces, and there was an equal amount either side. Except now there was this new piece, fist sized, between us on the table. I asked her if she knew what it was, and she did.

I asked her what she thought it was.

"It's that you want to have children."

"Oh," I said. I tried to say it in a way that made it smaller, that shrank the thing on the table into nothing, that made everything between us still even. But there's no changing what's true.

I picked it up. I had one of those moments where I knew what I was doing was wrong—terrible even—but I did it anyway. I held it out to her. "I think this one might be yours after all."

And she took it. She placed it in the box with the others. And then a bunch of things happened after that, things that I could tell you. About the other ones, the larger and larger pieces that kept turning up, their crushing weight, how they strained the drawstring of my bag and kept her box propped open for each of us to see. But I don't know. The story seems told.

Walden

Henry David Thoreau says from his spot on the couch, "What is once well done is done forever, Claire."

I stare straight ahead while I crack the eggs into the pan. The back-splash of my oven is covered in grease and flecks of crusted spaghetti sauce. *Tell him to get lost, Claire. Tell him to get his ass off the couch and get a goddam job. Tell him it's over.* I say nothing.

"Claire?"

"Go back to sleep."

He comes stumbling into the kitchen scratching idly at his stom-ach in my Joy Division shirt. He's a scrawny one, but it still bothers me that we wear the same size. Plus he's got a head like a sack of potatoes and tugs clothes on carelessly.

"Don't wear my things. I told you."

He looks down at the logo on it, as if he'd just noticed, and shrugs. "I like to smell of you."

I push the eggs around the pan with a spatula and ignore him. He comes up behind me.

"I was up with the dawn and didn't want to wake you, so I grabbed what was in arm's reach."

"Still. It's my shirt. And I heard you."

"Scrambled?"

"Yes."

"Just in the pan like that?"

"Yes."

"I've found that whisking them with a little milk beforehand makes a better texture."

"It might."

He sighs and pours himself some coffee. Yesterday's newspaper is spread over the kitchen table, and he sits to read, perched forward with his head supported by his hands. I'd subscribed to it as a kindness to him—not even my parents still read an actual physical newspaper. This was before I realized that Henry David Thoreau, my Henry David Thoreau, was a goony fucking mooch that would sit on my couch most of the day being alternately fascinated and horrified by daytime television and the 24-hour news cycle. About once a week at work I get a voicemail from him full of stentorian yelling.

We met at a bar a few miles down the road in Denton. I'd gone to school there, and then hung around for a time until I found a good enough job halfway between Denton and Dallas that seemed like the beginning steps of adulthood without really being a full commitment to the project of growing up. The bar was a converted house off the main square, and the entire backyard had been turned into a huge open-air patio. It was an unseasonably warm winter Saturday, and I met some friends from college up there. He came and sat down at a table with us after we'd had a few drinks and fell into the conversation with ease—it was that kind of place. My friends thought it was hilarious that he was Henry David Thoreau. They treated it as a joke. I was charmed, and though I maybe didn't believe him, I wanted to. He talked of making things of your own, of what it is to be connected to the land, of his brother the pencil-maker. Later, when we were kissing against my car, he said my name with a reverence, like he was glad it was me out of everyone. I had his complete attention. A rare enough thing, for me and everybody.

I scrape the eggs into two bowls and hand him one. We eat in silence, him absorbed in the paper, me leaning against the kitchen counter. There are dishes in the sink that I don't have time enough for. I look around to find my keys and then I'm out the door, into the thick Dallas morning.

I work in the last cubicle of a row that's five deep, up on the fourth floor of an anodyne beige office building. I have the choice spot—it's up against the window, and no one has any reason to walk by except to see me. It's a space I have fought and scrapped for through other people's pregnancies and transfers, even one person's death. I like to think of this as my making the best of a temporary situation. There are no pictures on my desk, no signs of me aside from my lunch in a Tupperware and my actual physical presence. I have a view of my Saab in the parking lot, and that's a great comfort to me.

Being team leader is mindless work that mostly involves being at my desk and ready to deal. Everything I do is just reacting. A thing I'm starting to think is leaking into my life. Like everyone here, I used to be a whole other person.

This morning, an email was waiting in my inbox that used the phrase, *There is no reason to be concerned*. The word *streamlining* appeared, as did *efficiency*. All day I have been looking up to see a new pair of coffee-cupped hands held close to the chest—my whole team right now is mousy women in Old Navy sweaters who stand as if they're trying to collapse into themselves. I answer their questions in my most reassuring voice. All of this is news to me, I say, and if something were really worth worrying about, I would know. I try not to say it with a pinched face.

Max shows up while I'm licking the last of my yogurt off of a spoon.

"Hey," he says.

"Look, Max. I am eating lunch at my desk. I am productive and efficient. I am streamlined."

Max and I ignore how much we don't like each other ever since I told him he had a dog's name and then asked if he was maybe named after a dog. It bothers him that I see this job for what it is, meaning necessary to my survival. At meetings, he says we are a family.

"I can see that. Good initiative, Claire."

I do not roll my eyes. I say, "What do you need?"

"Listen," he says, putting one butt cheek on my work space, "Did you see the article in the paper about us?"

"No. But I saw the email and have a brain."

"Well, what are you telling people?"

"I'm telling people not to worry."

"Okay, good," he says. Then he says it again, to himself.

"Should I be telling them different?"

"No. It's good, Claire." He stands up and gets partway down the aisle before turning back to me.

I call after him. "What?"

"Nothing. Just... nothing."

When I walk through the door, Henry David is playing Tetris in a chair I got from my grandparents' house after they went to the retirement home. I stand over him and put my hands on the chair back.

"You found my Game Boy."

He looks up at me without actually looking all the way up at me. "It's fascinating, but I worry about all this dependence people have on technology."

"Why's that?"

"Boredom can be important," he says, but he hasn't stopped playing. I wait for him to elaborate and he doesn't. I flick him on the top of the head and walk into the kitchen. The dishes are still there, the blame. They make me think about the possibility of losing my job, which I'd managed to put aside all day. The meaty fist of possible unemployment wraps my heart up for a second, gives it a hard squeeze.

"David," I call, "can you just—can you clean up when I'm gone?"

I look in the fridge. There's nothing much in there. "And can you go to the grocery store tomorrow?"

"Yes, but I don't have money."

"I'll leave money and a list. You want a grilled cheese and some soup?"

"Yes, darling."

I crinkle my nose, unwrap the cellophane from some single-slice cheese, and get a pan going on the stove. The soup stands firm and can-shaped in the pot until I stir it around. It's the dinner of a four-year-old, which I try not to think about.

He comes padding into the kitchen and picks up the cheese wrappers. "All this plastic," he says, and clucks his tongue.

"Well, recycle it." I don't tell him it's cellophane and probably not recyclable.

"I intend to."

"Ok then."

"I miss Walden," he says. "You know, I grew much of my own food there."

"I know," I say, flipping a grilled cheese. "Everybody knows."

He stands there like a child lost in the grocery store. I scratch at some of the spaghetti sauce stuck to the surface of my stove, and it gets jammed hard up under my fingernail. Then I let myself say something.

"What are you even doing with your life besides telling me what I'm doing wrong with mine? You and your fucking privilege."

He looks at me blank-faced, like he might cry, those sad, alive eyes set into his daguerreotype features going right past me.

"What?" I say.

"I am only trying to do good."

"Yeah, well," I say as I plate up his grilled cheese, "look around. It's not doing any good."

I hold out the grilled cheese for him. He reaches past it to pick up the soup can and the cellophane and throws them both in the garbage.

"There. That's how you want me to be. Waste and waste and waste."

I push the edge of the grilled cheese plate into his chest. "Eat your goddamn grilled cheese." I walk past him with my own plate and bowl of soup. "And maybe next time you want to be passive aggressive, don't announce it. That's aggressive aggressive."

He joins me at the table. "What do you want, Claire? A wooden man who does things without considering them?"

A long moment passes between us. I scowl at my soup. "What I want," I say softly, "is a normal fucking person for a fucking boyfriend, with a fucking job, and a fucking commute. I want someone who doesn't rub my nose in the fact that they get to be the kind of person they exactly imagine themselves to be while I'm over here with my mortgage and my car payment and my student loans."

He stands up in a huff and storms off into the bedroom, and I can hear him sniffling in there. After a minute he says, "If you want me to leave, you can say so. Trying to belittle me is just cruel."

I sigh. The truth is I don't know if I want him to leave, but I definitely want him to feel like I want him to leave. More than that, I want him to be Henry David Thoreau, the one who kisses like he means it, or the one who wrote what he wrote, either, or both, or whatever. This, though, this whiner, this thinker who doesn't do anything, it's too much.

"Look, that's not what I'm saying. I just need some help around here. I'm sorry. I'm really stressed with this thing at work."

The bed groans and he comes back in, rubbing at his face.

"I can do more," he says. I point at the chair, and he sits down to eat.

"I just don't understand why you're sitting around the house all day. You're Henry David Thoreau. Don't spin your wheels like this."

"You're right, of course." His eyes are downcast, and he chews his sandwich deliberately.

"I mean, I don't know. You should be writing, or doing something political. Or making something. You know?"

"I suppose so."

"Well, my mom always said you have to get out there and chase your happiness."

"I will." He reaches across the table to grip my arm. "Claire, I will." He seems to mean it, and he lets himself smile a bit.

I feel a little reassured. He's listening to me, he's thinking about his life. Maybe things can work out after all. I smile at him, a tentative warmth between us.

After dinner, I sit on the couch, and he comes over with a bottle of wine and two mugs. The way he sets the mugs down, opens the wine, pours it—there's a graciousness to it, a careful attention, the goodness that's always there in him. I know that in a minute, he'll kiss me, and I'll let him, and then he'll move into me while kissing me until I lay down on the couch, and then other things will happen, and that afterwards I'll feel alone and a little hard toward him, and if he asks me what's wrong, I'll lie.

In the morning, he's up before I am. I stumble out in a shirt and underwear to find all the windows thrown open and coffee brewed. Henry David is outside, framed by the window, scratching at his beard and staring hard at the lawn.

I pull on some pants, grab coffee, and walk out there. He turns toward me, his face brightening. "Claire!" he says. "I hope I didn't wake you. You were right, of course, that I need to consider who I am. I've been needing this."

"Needing what?"

"A new Walden!" He walks the lawn, heel-to-toe, as if he's measuring something.

"Figuratively speaking, of course."

"Of course!" He is beaming. He winks at me.

Inside, the morning's paper is spread out on the table. My company's name is on the front page. The layoffs rumors have gone airborne. I ignore it.

"I'm getting started straight away. I already ate breakfast," he says.

"That's good, Henry. It's good. There's a difference between living simply and living directionlessly, and—"

I turn around, and he's wandered back outside, leaving the door open behind him. I write down some stuff we need on a piece of scratch paper and leave it on the table with some cash.

There's another email at work. The language has taken on a desperate, grim tone. By ten in the morning the CFO has resigned. By lunchtime the usual murmur of office chatter has become loud and manic as a gaggle of employees hover by the community break area drinking generic soda. I use the time to get ahead on my quarterly reports, because surely we can't all be fired, and surely those of us who keep our mouths shut and our work impressive might be up for one of the jobs that has an office with a door.

In the early afternoon, I return from the bathroom to find Max sitting against the wall by my window. He looks crumpled, tossed there.

"Max."

"Claire, uh."

"Max, I'm trying to keep my head very deeply in the sand here, and you sitting on the floor is not helping."

He stands up and leans on my desk, stares out the window. I wait. He turns toward me and takes a pen out of my company coffee mug and runs it across his palm. It's a nice gel pen, so it leaves a thick smear on his skin.

"I bring those from home, Max."

He looks despondent. I think he might be drunk.

"Did you read the paper today?"

"Nope. I avoid it as a matter of policy."

"Has Henry told you about it? I know he follows the news."

"Don't talk to me about Henry, okay?"

"Why not?"

"Just don't, okay?"

He looks back out the window. "Okay, I'm going to tell you some-thing, and I want you to tell me if I'm fucked."

I log on to my computer and mime working.

"Say... say that maybe someone in our IT department uncovered a massive security loophole with the way our software processes credit card transactions, and say that maybe someone brought that info to me, and I told them to close the loophole, but then in the course of my other work I forgot to authorize the code for the version update that went out a few months ago, and say that then maybe it's possible that someone walked off with fifty or so million of our customer's credit card numbers as a result of that oversight, and, say, that, hey, it's an honest mistake, and—"

I turn to Max and he stops.

"Well, am I fucked or what?"

I look down the row of cubicles. "Who knows about this?"

"Nobody yet. But it's all there in my email and the workflows."

"Max."

"Yeah?"

"You're fucked."

When I get home he's out there in the front yard sitting on a fif-ty-pound bag of mulch with a rake balanced on his knees. There's a large, ragged rectangle on the lawn where the grass has been torn up and turned over. In the context of the neighborhood and its lush landscaped yards it's obscene, the dry bare earth of Texas out in the open like that. Spread out in front of him like a fanned deck of cards are little packets of seeds.

"What are you doing?"

"Thinking how best to plant these."

"I see that. And where did you get the money for the rake and the mulch and whatever else?"

We both already know the answer to this. He looks away and starts twisting his beard between his fingers.

"Goddammit Henry."

"We'll have no need for groceries in a few months. I bought enough seed for—"

"I don't give a shit how much seed you bought, or how we're gonna be swimming in zucchini, or what it is to grow something with your own hands. I care about groceries, and eating, today and tomorrow and the tomorrow after that." I am standing over him and pointing and yelling like a feral mother and I don't like any of it.

"Oh, Claire."

"Don't start. Don't even try and tell me anything. We live in a system. Get over it."

"I thought it would be fun. For both of us."

He looks dopey then, like a sad cartoon duck. I realize he's probably been waiting on me to get home, hoping that I'd want to help. He spins the rake in his lap, looking cute doing this, but also misguided and sad. He might be in love with me, and that's kind of awful and also heartening in a way that makes me queasy. I grab him by the shoulders.

"Henry. This is not helpful. The world doesn't work this way. I get why you're doing this, but you just can't."

"What else can I do?"

"I don't know. You've got to find a way to be useful."

"This is useful."

"No, Henry, it's not." I sit down in front of him on the grass. "Look, I go to the grocery store, I buy food. Everything beyond that—how it got there, where it was grown—that stuff is basically magic. I don't know anything about it. And I don't need to know."

"That's awful, Claire."

I look past him to the wound in my yard. "I know it is. But what can you do?"

"Plenty. You can't let other people do your surviving for you."

"I can, and I do."

He lets out a long, shuddering sigh. His hands are dirt-caked. I reach out and drag a nail down one of them, leaving a thin, clean line.

"Look," I say. "I like you, Henry. I like all this. But it's time to tell me. It's an act."

"What is?"

"This." I wave my hand in front of his face. "The garden, the beard, all of it. This whole thing."

His face turns sour with rage. He stands up, throws down the rake, and storms down the street. I watch him go, call half-heartedly after him. It's a shock, but also I guess not, because why would I say a thing like that unless I wanted something like this to happen?

I don't see him for the rest of the night. I feel guilty about it, but also it's peaceful, my space feels like my own, and I order dinner out, and I watch a show about rich people being horrible, and I turn up Patti Smith's "Land" on my record player and dance around shouting, "*Horses! Horses! Horses!*" while spilling gin and soda on the carpet, and all night, no one says anything about it.

The next morning I'm hung over at work. It feels about the same as usual, but I must be feeling vulnerable, or at least susceptible to kindness, because when Max comes over with his loose-knotted tie and his flop-sweated everything I don't even have it in me to make fun of him or give him the boot. Though I could get away with it. Probably I could get away with anything, knowing what I know.

"I need to, uh, I need your discretion. On what we talked about."
He looks out the window instead of at me, but he's turned toward
me, like looking out the window is just something he's doing and
not a deliberate avoidance.

"You got it, Max. I don't want anything to do with anything." I'd
been holding a Diet Dr. Thunder from the fridge, and I press my cold
palm against my forehead. It feels nice. I close my eyes.

"No, I mean it."

"Yeah, me too."

A second goes by. I'm in the dark behind my closed eyes. Nothing
can get at me in here.

"Claire."

"Look, I pinky swear, or it's a blood oath, or whatever holds up
best in a court of law. Just leave me alone, okay?"

"No, you need to look at this."

I open my eyes and he's pressed all the way up against the window,
looking down. I stand up and walk over to him. Out the window, in
the parking lot near my Saab, is Henry David. He's holding a sign that
says, "Men first. Subjects afterward." There are a few other people
I don't recognize out there with him, and they're lounging around
like they're waiting on more before starting whatever it is they're
going to start.

"Ah, shit," I say.

Max, god bless him, busts out laughing. He slaps the glass twice with
his palm and wanders off. Down below more people are walking up.

By noon they are organized and marching, about twenty in all. The
next day there are a few more. On Friday, the local news is out there
for an hour. I watch the report that night, and the anchor is baffled
by it all, since the only thing they know currently is that there are
rumors of impending layoffs, nothing confirmed.

I send an email about moving them out of the parking lot, at least. I pretend I'm concerned about vandalism of cars. I get a response from Toby in security asking if I really think my boyfriend is going to key my car, so I drop it. Meanwhile people around me aren't doing their work. Instead, they're putting together their résumés, taking long lunches, while I sit here in my undecorated cubicle. I don't have to tell them to do any of this—they can smell it. As soon as Max's fuck up gets traced back to our team, well, I'm sure it will be swift, whatever it is.

I could've put something up in my space. A photo, a little cactus in a ceramic cowboy boot, a plastic flamingo like Janet down the row. Something to prove I was here after I'm laid off.

On Saturday morning, I wake up to Henry in the front yard. He's finishing the work on the garden. I watch him out the window with coffee in my hand. He sees me, and I wave a little bit, though I'm mad as shit at him, and part of me wants him to light himself on fire in the office parking lot. At least then he'll be interesting. I'm not typically a violent or dark-thoughted person, but this is what he does to me.

I feel guilty, so I pour him a cup of coffee, too, though it's already too hot out for it. He takes it from me anyway.

"You've been busy," I say.

"I suppose so." He takes a sip and sets it down in the grass nearby before going back to turning over the earth. "Save me the coffee grounds, if you would. We'll put them to use out here."

He sees the look on my face and deflates. "I'll get these planted. Spread your coffee grounds over them as mulch. Then it's just a matter of watering and checking in on the seedlings. You might have to get some herbicide or natural repellants. The internet can tell you a lot of the rest, I'm sure."

"Okay, Henry."

"It's worth doing," he says, bending down to put his hand in the dirt.

"Okay." I can see why people would believe him, but looking down at him there on my lawn, I just don't. Mostly I feel lousy, like I'm mad that I was naïve, or I'm mad that I can't be naïve any more. They're the same feeling, really.

On Monday, the story hits about Max's mistake and we're national news. When the guy who's supposed to re-stock the break room every week doesn't show up, I know it's over. Down in the parking lot, Henry's little group of protesters has tripled in size.

Max walks up while I'm watching out the window. I say, "I mean, we're fuck-ups. A terrible company in the process of going under. But why do these people care enough to be out there?"

"I don't know. He's your boyfriend."

"I'm talking about the rest of them. Henry makes perfect sense."

"I guess they just feel betrayed is all."

"Betrayed by who?"

"Us. Everything. Me, I guess."

I look over at him. He's not my friend, but at least I get a sense of him as a human being now instead of as an extension of a corporate ideology.

"You should screw up more often. It makes you more likable."

He gives me a tepid smile. "You're fired, Claire."

Henry has got a megaphone now, and he's shouting something up at us. From behind glass it comes out as a low drone. People behind him pump their fists.

"I know." I reach over and tighten up his tie, which was hanging loose and ugly on him. "So are you. At least you deserve it. At least for you it'll make some sense."

He presses an index finger onto the glass at the protesters so hard it goes white. "Fuck these little limp shits." Then he turns to me. "Sorry."

"Don't be sorry." I say, and I pat him on the arm. Then I turn around and grab my purse, my car keys, my lukewarm coffee. Some of my co-workers look up, but none of them stop me. The elevator is on my floor already, so there's no wait, and in the lobby I give Toby, the security guy, a wave.

He calls out, "Do you want me to have him arrested?"

And I say, "I'd say yes if he wouldn't love it so much."

I walk past all of them without making eye contact. To their credit, they don't mob me or yell. Henry says my name into the megaphone once, though. I don't stop. I'm in my car. I'm pulling out of the space. I'm going home to see whether or not I can make an honest thing happen. I'm going home to tend my garden.

Social Animals

Our hearts, at least, were raised by wolves. Say what you might about our manners, which were impeccable, or our charm, which was not insignificant, or the way we lit up the room, the two of us. Get out of the room, leave us in there on our own, and it wouldn't be long until we were all snapping jaws. It wasn't so much that we fought as that everything we did devoured, even when we were trying to be kind. Sometimes we would make love like we were trying to fuck each other gone. And we drank. We drank to lick our wounds, and we drank for the courage to go for the throat, though neither of us had the kind of forethought to see it that way. Mostly we just drank: escape, crutch, fear, love, chemical imbalances, the whole of who we were or could possibly hope to be. I don't make apologies.

Eventually, my family would get wind of how run-ragged we were and send me to a drying out place. She went with me once, but mostly it was me out in Waco feeling lousy and like I didn't deserve the life I had. None of it. Sometimes, I would think about dying when I was at those places, but you got to do a whole thing to get that done, and I was never much of a planner. Anyhow it seemed selfish, and I only felt that way clean. A symptom of the cure.

She would call every day, then every other day, then every now and again. I told her I didn't mind, though I did. I minded like crazy, seeing as I couldn't stomach talking to anyone else. I've always been way cooler of policy than of heart. That's the way of most people, I guess.

I thought about getting religion the last time. I mean I prayed here and there. To be honest, I got more out of talking to a stray dog that hung around, this old dusty deadeye thing. All told, I might put talking to him ahead of the phone calls, too. Some things you can never really be sure of. Anyway, I was lonely.

Those four weeks would bring with them a kind of clarity, but rarely the kind I wanted. Something between freedom and a certain lush sadness was what I was after. But this place had a way of making you feel like a bird looking at his gnarled and knotty feet, as though that's the point of a bird. As though your scars are supposed to matter when you're in the air, when alighting on a branch is not a thing you ever intend to do. As though I didn't know how I got here, that it's just the trap of being alive when what you're made for is the wind, when that's what love is and family is and home is, when what you're made for and can never actually be is here and also gone.

Hypotheticals

A person wakes up one morning to find that they are sad. This is not news, as a person is often sad. The sadness that a person feels does not require a reason, but a person, being rational, seeks one anyway. And then, from there, maybe a solution could be looked for.

It might happen like this: a person sits up in bed, prepares to live a whole day, uses a cell phone to watch a video of a dog eating pizza, and then is forced to reckon with their sadness. A person might wonder how universal their experience is without that universality—or lack thereof—causing a further wrinkle to the sadness that they experience. This is, of course, allowed and possible and even happens, sometimes. A person might suppose that focusing on the universality of experience might even be a kind of solution to sadness. Though in some—even many—cases it isn't.

Or else a person might rise immediately, skipping the phone-in-bed part of the morning, looking for the dew-dappled new feeling of young daylight. In that case, there might be something in the air worth breathing in, or streaks of yellow pollen on all the cars, or actual chirping birds—birds not existing only as the providence of the proverbial—or just a chance at seeing people dressed nicely for work or school might be enough to cause a forgetting of sadness. A person might need only to forget for a minute for the sadness to be gone. Sadness might be as fleeting as joy.

If not, though, a person might search for places to go on vacation. A person might stay in playing videogames all day, claiming illness. A person might masturbate or have sex with a stranger, might take sadness out for a drive or might just take sadness out on someone else. A person might get a hermit crab at a store in a beach community and make it a little beachy home in a plastic terrarium bought for that purpose. There's so much a person might do, each *if* so crowded with *thens*. And is this abundance a part of the sadness, or is it rather that out of that abundance only one thing ever happens?

Finally, a person might invent for themselves some kind of framing device to bracket off the things that they feel into discrete units of meaning. They might make a list of reasons they feel sad and reasons they shouldn't. They might spreadsheet or bullet journal the mess of feeling until it reveals its way to be clean. They might write a story, even, that puts their sadness at such a remove that they no longer have to hold on to it. Imagine that. Imagine a person so foolish and desperate.

When a person arrives at the beach community, they might stop at a lunch stand and order a sandwich and two kinds of chips. They might wonder how they would write it all down. Is it a west coast beach or an east coast beach? It doesn't much matter, probably, except in the brand of chips available, in the particular texture of décor. Are there surfers, or are there retirees walking their black labs? Are there rocks, driftwood, the placental bag of a dead jellyfish, a kind of life so foreign as to be unrecognizable and new to a person? Will a person meet someone? Will a person convince a friend to come along? Will a person feel connected to nature or to people or to god/existence/their own eager self? And what of the sun in the sky? Will it be beautiful today? Will a person find it beautiful? And can someone here tell me if there's a next?

Acknowledgements

I would like to extend my thanks to the journals that have published portions of this book either online or in print: "Accord" in *The Adroit Journal*, "The Artist Requires Your Dissent" in *Portland Review*, "City Council" in *Passages North*, "Flood Myth" in *Bop Dead City*, "Full Bloom" in *Hot Street*, "Imperative" in *Heavy Feather Review*, "Hypotheticals" in *Okay Donkey*, "In Ocala" in *decomP*, "Kinds of Rubble" in *Thin Air*, "Lost or Found" in *Gettysburg Review*, "Luck" in *Bodega Magazine*, "Reveal" in *Pidgeonholes*, "Spite House" in *Necessary Fiction*, "Status Updates" in *Ninth Letter*, "A Testimony" in *Crack the Spine*, "Tucumcari" in *Slice Magazine*, and "Walden" in *PRISM International*. That people have the drive and passion to bring stories forth into this world at all is a miracle, and that those same people believed in my stories is a true honor. That's true times a million for the team at Mason Jar, who have been the kindest, smartest collaborators I've ever had the pleasure of working with.

I'd also like to thank my Denton family for being there for me through the writing of many of these stories and for helping me learn who I am (particularly everyone at Spiderweb Salon), and I'd like to thank my DC family for giving me home and community and patiently listening when I explain that the movie we're watching is a satire, actually. The love and shelter I've had along the way are immeasurable.

And to Jaclyn: without you, I simply would not be here at all. Thank you for your patience, for listening to these stories as they came to be, and for never doubting me along the way. Let's keep going!

About the Author

Zach VandeZande is a lapsed Texan living in Burlington, VT with a partner and a dog. He is the author of *Apathy and Paying Rent* (Loose Teeth Press, 2008) and *Liminal Domestic: Stories* (Gold Wake Press, 2019), and his work has appeared in *Ninth Letter*, *Split Lip*, *Georgia Review*, *DIAGRAM*, and other journals. He got his PhD at the University of North Texas, where he also learned the value of hammocks and baking bread. He knows all the dogs in his neighborhood.

Other Titles From Mason Jar Press

JERKS
short stories by Sara Lippmann

The Monotonous Chaos of Existence
short stories by Hisham Bustani

Peculiar Heritage
poetry DeMisty D. Bellinger

Call a Body Home
short stories chapbook by Michael Alessi

The Horror is Us
an anthology of horror fiction edited by Justin Sanders

Suppose Muscle Suppose Night Suppose This in August
memoir by Danielle Zaccagnino

Ashley Sugarnotch & the Wolf
poetry by Elizabeth Deanna Morris Lakes

...and Other Disasters
short stories by Malka Older

Learn more at masonjarpress.com